Flame swept across the tops of the trees from northwest to northeast. Less than three hundred yards upslope, both roads were invisible beneath dense coagulations of smoke. Growing wider and hungrier by the second, the blaze was already spread out before them like a gigantic wall a thousand yards long.

Wildfire.

And both roads to safety impassably blocked . . .

Any second now there was going to be mass panic.

Sam Honeycutt could see it in the faces of the men and women around him, feel it clogging the air as thickly as the scorching firewind and the choking smoke. And if it were allowed to ignite, it would spread with the same destructive speed of the fire.

Trapped, we're t

Also by Bill Pronzini
Published by Ballantine Books:

THE HANGINGS

THE LAST DAYS OF HORSE-SHY HALLORAN

QUINCANNON

THE GALLOWS LAND

FIREWIND

Bill Pronzini

BALLANTINE BOOKS • NEW YORK

Library of Congress Catalog Card Number: 88-33578

ISBN 0-345-36529-1

This edition published by arrangement with M. Evans and Company, Inc.

Manufactured in the United States of America

First Ballantine Books Edition: June 1990

CHAPTER 1

1

It was some past noon when they climbed the last long stretch of wagon road to the rim of Big Tree Valley.

The Espenshied freighter had developed a hot axle and screeched like a banshee all the way up the grade. The noise had set Clee Rudabaugh's teeth on edge. But there was no place along the narrow road for Morley Patch, the teamster he'd recruited in San Francisco, to pull off so he could grease the axle from the tar bucket. Now, along the rim where the road leveled off and widened out for a space before it began its descent, Patch halted the six-yoke ox team and the screeching along with it. The sweltering silence was like a balm on Rudabaugh's tortured eardrums.

Patch and Chavis both took out bandannas and wiped their sweating faces. Chavis said, "Christ, it's hot," and spat down among the oxen.

Rudabaugh had nothing to say. Talking to these two was a chore at the best of times, and he avoided conversation unless it was necessary. Patch was taciturn by nature, nervous at times, and slow to use his wits, but he could handle a freighter better than anybody Rudabaugh had ever seen—and that was vital on these narrow mountain roads. Besides which, he took orders without back talking. Chavis took orders, too, up to a point. He was a hulking, mean-spirited dullard, not much brighter than the oxen pulling the Espenshied. Rudabaugh had known him since before the war, when they'd both

1

ridden with a band of freebooters posing as Regulators during the trouble between Free Soilers and pro-slavery factions on the Kansas-Missouri border. They'd looted villages and farms, riding by night to avoid the genuine peacekeepers, and got away with it fine until the army sent in extra troops.

Chavis began rolling one of his loose cigarettes, dribbling tobacco down the front of his hickory shirt. You'd think that a man who had lived more than forty years would have learned how to roll a tight smoke. Rudabaugh quit looking at him, watched Patch—heavyset, plodding, with whiskers so thick they grew down his neck under his collar—get down off the high seat and move out of sight to the rear of the wagon. Than he took the spyglass from under the seat and got down himself.

He stretched cramped muscles, went along the rutted hardpan of the road to where a cluster of rocks rose like a small watchtower. He climbed the rocks, taking his time about it. He didn't have to go all the way to the top before he commanded an unobstructed view of the valley spread out below.

Heat haze shimmered above it like a layer of smoke. Some of it *was* smoke, he saw then, coming from inside the big, fenced mill compound off north. Behind the sawmill, a big mushroom-shaped chip burner was sending up thick plumes that flattened and spread out when they hit the layer of haze, same as against something solid. If there'd been a breeze, you would be able to smell the wood smoke up here; but there was no breeze. It was hot, all right. This was northern California mountain country, but it was desert-hot just the same.

He fitted the spyglass to his right eye, adjusted the focus. He scanned the valley first, fixing it all in his mind. The mill was at the north end, where the only two roads intersected—tucked into the wedge formed by the roads as if it were filling in a fat slice of pie. The company town, Big Tree, fanned out to the south, what there was of it. One-block main street, a couple of side streets, thirty or forty houses and cabins extending partway up the wooded hillside to the east. The feeder railroad spur angled in through a cut in the hills at the south end, passed through a yard section and over east of Main Street, and then through the wide front gates of the mill compound. In the yard section there was a roofed platform and a small work building, a water tower, and two short sidings. A small locomotive was on one of the sidings, drawn up beneath the water tower; on the other siding were a pair of boxcars and a couple of old passenger coaches that looked as if they would shake apart in a stiff wind. That was about all there was to see, other than trees and hills—some of the hill flanks logged bare except for stumps and tangles of slash and second-growth timber—and jutting mountain scarps in the distance.

Rudabaugh gave his attention to the mill. Big Tree Lumber Company. Austin Trace, Proprietor. He smiled thinly as he scanned the big sawmill, the storage sheds, the ricks of logs and sawn lumber, the conical mounds of sawdust and chips; the rail tracks and yard engine; the workers moving here and there at their jobs. On the near side of the hill above the compound was the house from where Austin Trace could look down on everything he owned. Especially on the big storage building not far away, where the munitions were supposed to be. All of it was enclosed by redwood fencing eight feet high, more as a barrier against prying eyes than to keep out intruders.

Everything seemed to tally with the map in Rudabaugh's pocket, and with what he'd been told by Untermeyer and Duggan. But after they found a place to make camp, he'd go down for a closer look. There were a few things he needed to find out before they went after the cache.

Rudabaugh sectioned the spyglass and climbed down off the rocks, again taking his time. Above the haze of heat and smoke, the sky was a cloudless blue. If it stayed that way, there'd be a moon tonight. In and out in less than eighteen hours—that would be the ideal way to do it.

In poor and out rich. The thought made Rudabaugh smile his thin smile. In poor and out rich—thirty thousand dollars rich. When Untermeyer paid off, it would be the most money he'd ever held at one time, by a damn sight.

Still smiling, he went back to the freighter, where Patch

was greasing the hot axle and Chavis was pissing on the road next to the off-wheel ox.

2

When Matt Kincaid road down the east slope into town, he spied Sam Honeycutt over in the rail yard. There was nobody else around and he felt the need of some conversation; he rode on down Main Street to where Honeycutt was sitting in the shade alongside the work building, doing something to a section of track switch. The cold nub of a short-six seegar protruded from under the old man's droopy, tobacco-stained mustache. At Kincaid's approach, he glanced up and a smile creased his wrinkled hound's face.

"Afternoon, Matt."

"Sam."

Kincaid dismounted, tied his horse, and sat down. Stretched his long legs out in front of him and took off his hat. His shaggy red hair was damp with sweat. He ran a hand through it, then took out his kerchief and mopped his face and neck. "Hot," he said.

"Ain't it. Fire weather."

"Now that'd be all we need."

"Drought, heat, dry timber—we been plenty lucky not to've had a fire around here." Honeycutt paused. "They ain't so lucky over to Pine Hill."

"Fire over that way?"

"Started yesterday. Word come over the wire this morning."

Despite his sixty-odd years, Honeycutt held down a number of duties in Big Tree. One of them was telegrapher. He also saw to track and rail equipment repairs, served as a fill-in engineer on the Springwood run if the need arose. He had worked in railroading for forty years, mostly on the Union Pacific back in Kansas and Nebraska, until a dispute with a division super put him out of work. He'd come out here then, because he had kin in California, and got himself hired by Austin Trace.

Kincaid chewed at his underlip, thinking that Pine Hill

was only thirty miles away to the northeast. He asked, "Out of control?"

"Yep. And likely to stay that way. Weather like this, any forest fire's too wild to tame."

"Any chance it'll spread this far?"

Honeycutt shook his head. "Not enough fuel. But it'll do a hell of a lot of damage before it burns itself out. Two thousand acres gone already, all prime timberland."

A silence built between them. Kincaid was no longer thinking about the fire damage; he had too many other things on his mind to add another worry. He sat half watching a sixteen-mule team come down the east road, hauling a freighter with a pair of back-actions coupled behind it; all three wagons swayed under loads of high-piled logs. Bells suspended above the bearskin housings of each mule's collar made clear, steady sounds in the overheated air. He listened to the bells until one of the bullwhackers commenced to shouting and cussing and cracking his blacksnake, and then the mill's steam saw drowned out all of it in a long, keening shriek as the five-foot circular blades bit into another log.

A woman came walking out of one of the side streets onto Main, a market basket over one arm. Kincaid sat forward to squint against the sun-glare. But the woman wasn't Rose Denbow.

He leaned back again. Hell of a way for a grown man to act, he chided himself for maybe the hundredth time. But knowing it and putting a stop to it were two different things. She was on his mind night and day now. He was in love with her, no denying that. And there wasn't a damned thing he could do about it, except to stay clear of her and wait for the flame to die down, if it ever would.

He was plenty of things, but a wife stealer wasn't one of them.

He shook himself, considered filling his pipe, decided it was too hot to smoke, and thought about moving on to the company store for the supplies he needed. Instead he sat slouched on the bench and asked Honeycutt, "You got that Baldwin ready for service yet?" Meaning the Baldwin locomotive on the siding behind them. Honeycutt had been tinkering with it for a year and a half now, six months longer than Kincaid had been in these mountains. It had been taken out of service at the mill because of an assortment of mechanical problems.

"Just about," the old man said. "Got her steam up two days ago, ran the gauge all the way up. She'll run. Question is, how far and how long?"

"How come she's still under the tower?"

"Figured I'd take her out tomorrow or the next day, downtrack a ways. See how she goes. If she don't give me any trouble, I'll take her all the way into Springwood. Have the chief mechanic and his crew take her into the roundhouse and give her a proper going-over."

"Then what?"

"Dunno yet. I'd like to keep her here, as a backup to that new Mallet at the mill. She'll probably end up in the Springwood yards, though." Honeycutt made a wry mouth. "Me, too, before I'm turned out to pasture."

"Doomsaying again, Sam?"

"Facts is facts," Honeycutt said. "Things at the mill worsen every day, seems like. Production's the lowest in ten years, and Trace just don't seem to give a damn. Talk is he's fixin' to lay off another eight to ten men."

"Why doesn't he sell out?"

"Don't ask me. He's had offers, I know that."

"He'll have to sell sooner or later, won't he?"

"You'd think so. Never know what a man like him will do, though. He just ain't been the same since his son got killed by the Nez Perce and his wife grieved herself to death. Warped him, losin' both of them three months apart. The mill ain't mattered to him since."

"Something must matter to him," Kincaid said. "He's been down to San Francisco three or four times lately."

"Beats me what it is. Thought maybe he'd been workin' out a deal to sell, but that don't seem to be it." Honeycutt took the seegar nub out of his mouth, scowled at it, and pitched it away into the dust. "If he don't sell, the mill's a goner—dead inside of two years, the way he's runnin' it now.

And if the mill dies, this town dies with it. We'll all be lookin' for new jobs and new places to live.''

"Me included," Kincaid said. "I can't sell my beef to bears and a scatter of Indians. My ranch won't be worth a plugged nickel.''

"Still think I'm doomsayin' for nothing?''

"I never thought that, Sam. I just keep hoping you're wrong.''

"No more than I do," Honeycutt said ruefully.

From where he sat, Kincaid could see past a couple of shade oaks to where the two sealed boxcars sat on the siding nearby, ahead of the passenger coaches that were kept here for emergencies and holiday runs to Springwood. He had noticed them when he rode in. He asked Honeycutt, "What's in the boxcars?''

"Machine parts, supposed to be.''

"Supposed to be?''

"Two full-loaded boxcars is a hell of a lot of machine parts.''

"They being shipped out?''

"Yep. Over to Springwood and then north somewheres. Ben Purdom brought 'em out on the Mallet yesterday. They're scheduled to go out on tomorrow's run.''

"Why would Trace be sending two carloads of machine parts up north?''

"Just what I asked Ben," Honeycutt said. "He didn't know. Said Trace had the cars loaded last night from a storage shed that's always kept under lock and key. Nobody allowed inside. Parts come in piecemeal, he said, and he can't recollect any of 'em ever bein' used. Funny, ain't it?''

"Some. Reckon he's selling off equipment to raise capital?''

"Could be.''

Kincaid shrugged. "Well, whatever's in those cars, I guess it's no particular business of ours.''

"No," Honeycutt agreed. "I guess it ain't, at that.''

3

Will Denbow sat on the edge of his bed, lips peeled in against his teeth, and began the ritual of strapping on his wooden leg.

It was made of hardwood, with a thick circlet of cotton batting inside the top, where it fitted over his stump, and a padded harness that fastened around the upper thigh. Denbow thought of it as a crutch, as something a man who had never leaned on anything or anybody was now forced to lean on for the rest of his life. It was a constant reminder that he was half a man, and he hated it. He hated it almost as much as he hated the smooth, round stump that ended above where the knee ought to be, all that was left of his right leg.

He didn't look at the stump as he strapped on the peg leg; he had quit looking at it not long after the accident six months before. That made the task of putting on the crutch difficult, but he didn't care about that. He kept his eyes on the open window across the bedroom, fumbling with the harness, getting it cinched into place awkwardly by feel. A faint breeze, thick with the smell of pine pitch and resin, came in through the window but did not stir the stagnant air in the room. Even at four o'clock in the afternoon, the summer heat lay like a heavy blanket over the valley.

Pustules of sweat dotted Denbow's face. He paused to draw an arm across his forehead, then finished buckling the harness and caught the wooden leg in both hands and jammed it hard into the stump; felt a sharp, satisfying cut of pain. Then, in clumsy movements, he pushed off the bed. Once he had his balance, he turned to the chair where his pants were.

Rose was standing in the bedroom doorway.

Denbow said irritably, "What the hell are you doing? You know I don't like you watching me put on the leg."

"I wasn't watching you. I've only been here a second."

"Well? What do you want?"

"Are you going out?"

"What do you think."

"I . . . wish you wouldn't."

"No? Why not?"

"I thought we might . . . well, you know."

"For God's sake. Is that all you think about?"

She winced. "Will, that's not fair."

"Isn't it?"

"You know it isn't. It has been more than two months. . . ."

"Hell it has. You keep track of things like that?"

"Why do you make me beg this way?"

"It's too damned hot," he said.

"You never used to think it was too hot."

"I never used to think a lot of things. I never used to have one leg, neither." He limped to the chair and struggled into his pants.

From the doorway Rose watched him. Her eyes were a pale blue, like blue velvet. He avoided them, just as he avoided looking at the stump of his right leg.

She said tentatively, "Will . . ."

"No, damn it," he said. "How come all this sudden need for loving, anyhow? Before the accident you weren't after me about it all the time."

"Before the accident we never went two months without each other."

"What is it with you? You *like* doing it with a one-legged man? You enjoy this stump of mine sliding around on top of you?"

She put a hand to her cheek as if he'd slapped her. "My Lord, what a thing to say?"

"Well? Do you?"

"You're being cruel."

He felt cruel, as cruel as life had been to him. He sang a verse of a dance-hall song, as he sometimes did, because he knew she hated it:

> "Oh, he married her, he married her.
>   How could he be so cruel?
> She was so poor, she had to use
>   His wooden leg for fuel!"

She turned before he was finished and fled to another room.

Denbow finished buttoning his pants. He clumped into the kitchen, pumped cold water into a basin, washed his face. In the mirror he used for shaving, he caught a glimpse of himself. Thick beard bristles made his cheeks look shadowed, made him look ten years older than thirty-one. To hell with that, too.

When he turned, Rose was there again. She said in a weary voice, "You're going to the saloon again, I suppose."

"What difference does it make where I go?"

"I wish you wouldn't drink so much—"

"What else is there for a cripple to do?"

"We could *talk*," she said.

"Sure. Talk about that job in the dispatcher's office down in Oakland, right?"

"It's a good job—"

"It's a miserable job," he said. "I'm not gonna sit behind some clerk's desk all day, shuffling papers. I couldn't stand it."

"Will, be reasonable. What other options do you have?"

"I'll get a tin cup," he said savagely, "and beg nickels on a street corner!"

"Won't you *ever* stop feeling sorry for yourself?"

He glared at her. Then he pushed past her, roughly, and stalked out to the front door. He heard Rose following, but he didn't look back at her. He jerked the door open and limped out onto the porch and started down the steps.

But he was too angry to pay proper attention to what he was doing. The tip of the wooden leg caught on one of the lower treads and sent him sprawling onto the path at the bottom.

He landed painfully on his hip and left elbow, rolled halfway onto his back. Above and behind him, Rose said, "Will!" and there was the slap of the door as she came out. She ran down the steps, bent over him with her hand extended.

A black rage had control of him now; he slapped her hand aside. "Leave me alone!" he shouted. "Get away from me!"

She flinched, backed up a step. Denbow struggled into a sitting position, got his good leg under him, and managed to heave himself erect. In one of the trees that flanked the house, a jay made a raucous cry, as if it were laughing at him. He could feel his face burning. He balled his fist and slammed it against the stump. Did it again. And again.

"Will, don't—"

He swung away from her, hobbled down the path to the front gate. Outside it, he stood staring through dusty sunlight and tree shadows at Main Street a block away. *You son of a bitch!* he thought. And drove his fist once more into the dead stump of his leg.

4

In his cluttered study, Austin Trace sat staring at the silver-framed photographs on his desk. He spent too much time staring at them, brooding over them—he knew that. But he did it, anyway. They were like magnets that drew him, held him, stirred his pain, sharpened his love, and fueled his hate.

Clara, apple-cheeked and smiling, with the bloom of youth still in her round face. The bloom that had faded and withered, until in just three months she was old, old, and there was nothing in the once-bright blue of her eyes except death. And Stephen, so young and handsome in his uniform, smiling, proud—Lieutenant Stephen Trace, on the day of his graduation from West Point. An officer and a gentleman, unlike his father, who had been a mere corporal in the cavalry and who had decided within a year of his own enlistment that his ambitions lay outside the military. Yes, an officer and a gentleman, with his whole fine life ahead of him.

Four brief months of life ahead of him.

June 17, 1877: a day of infamy. The day young Stephen, while on his first assignment under Brevet Colonel Perry, captain of the 1st Cavalry at Fort Lapwai in Idaho Territory, had died in a place called White Bird Canyon on the Clearwater River—one of thirty-four soldiers butchered in a surprise attack by the goddamned Nez Perce Indians.

That had been the beginning of the Nez Perce War, that unprovoked slaughter in White Bird Canyon. Unprovoked, yes, no matter what the heathen chiefs claimed about broken treaties. Some of the young bucks had set to murdering white settlers, hadn't they? Colonel Perry and the two companies of his regiment had every right to march on Looking Glass's camp, and every right to expect to be met in open combat rather than a vicious assault from ambush. Tired troops, thirty-six hours in the saddle from Fort Lapwai; unsuspecting troops, with their hands empty of weapons. Cut down, cut to ribbons, before they knew what was happening. Butchery. Stephen and thirty-three others, like steers in a slaughtering pen . . .

Four bloody months the war had raged. From the Clearwater to the Kamiah Crossing. Along the Lolo Trail over the Bitterroots. At the Big Hole River east of the Continental Divide. Across the Big Muddy at Cow Island near Fort Benton. And finally up into the Bear Paw Mountains. More fine, brave young soldiers killed, scores of them, including twenty-nine at Big Hole River, before General Mills put an end to it with six hundred troops, a Gatling run, and a twelve-pound Napoleon. The savages had surrendered on the fifth day of October, Chief Joseph making a speech that was reported in newspapers all along the Pacific Coast. "From where the sun now stands," the brute had said in conclusion, "I will fight no more."

Clara had been in her grave just three weeks when Trace learned of the surrender and read the words of Chief Joseph. Learned, too, that the government intended no further punishment of the savages for what they'd done. The wounds inside him had broken open all over again, to fester with the pus of his rage and hate. He made a vow of his own that day. "From where the sun now stands," he had said to the photographs of Stephen and Clara, "I'll not rest until Joseph and Ollokut and Looking Glass and all the rest of them are punished—until I see them punished with my own eyes for what they have done."

At first he had sought his vengeance through peaceable means, political means. It was only after his entreaties continued to be met with indifference and scorn that he had begun making his own plans. It had taken him the better part of three years, cost him most of his fortune, but now it was done. Three hundred hardbitten mercenary soldiers had been carefully recruited and were assembling now in Portland. Plans for his own surprise attack had been laid. All the necessary weaponry had been bought, brought here to Big Tree in small shipments, and was ready now for transit to Oregon. Once the arms arrived in Portland and his army of vengeance was ready, he would join them for the trek northward. He would kill Joseph himself, when the time came. He had thought of little else for more than a year now, dreamed of little else. Joseph would die by *his* hand, just as Stephen had died by Joseph's. An eye for an eye, a tooth for a tooth.

Abruptly Trace got to his feet—tall, dour, stoop shouldered—and crossed to the window that looked out over the mill and the town beyond. On the siding he could see the two sealed boxcars waiting for their journey north. Winchester .44–40s and Remington Rolling-Block .50s, two Gatling guns, a howitzer, cases of government-issue sidearms, many thousand rounds of ammunition, kegs of black powder, and boxes of dynamite. Enough firepower to ensure that every last Nez Perce—men, women, children, babes in arms—was obliterated from the face of the earth.

He watched mill workers scurrying at their jobs below, knew what they would say if they knew of his plans. They would say he was mad, that his vendetta against the Nez Perce must surely fail. But *he* knew differently. If the shipment of munitions reached Portland, then the plan would succeed. He believed that with all his heart and soul. And the shipment *would* get through, he assured himself again. It was a simple matter of transportation, of two sealed boxcars traveling by established short-line routes from point *A* to point *B*. There was no reason, none, for anyone to question the bills of lading or to open the cars en route.

Trace turned again, went back to his desk, once again picked up the photographs of his dead wife and dead son.

"Soon now, Stephen," he said softly. "Soon now, Clara. Soon."

What could possibly go wrong?

CHAPTER 2

1

ROSE DENBOW SAT AT THE TABLE IN HER KITCHEN, FIN-
ished with picking at another lonely supper. There were still
two hours of daylight left, but the trees outside made the
room dusky with shadow, and she had lighted a lamp. In its
flickery glow she read again the letter from her sister in San
Francisco, which had arrived the week before. She had put
off answering it, but tonight, with the pain of Will's cruelty
still lingering, she felt the need to unburden herself.

She cleared the table, brought paper and pen and ink. For
a time she sat staring at the paper, trying to arrange her
thoughts. Then she dipped the pen's nib into the ink bottle,
hesitated, and finally began to write.

Dear Meg,

I have your most recent letter. It is wonderful news that
you are expecting again. I know how much Edward wants
a son, and I hope you are able to give him one this time.
You seem so happy, I hesitate to burden you with my troubles. Yet I do not know what to do, and I beg your understanding and advice.

Meg, my marriage is dying. I do not know if I can save
it, or even if I want to save it, God help me. Will has
changed so much since the accident, you cannot imagine
what it has done to him and what he is doing to himself.
He is so full of self-pity, it is destroying him by inches.

He no longer loves me, I am certain of that. I wonder sometimes if he ever did—deeply, as I loved him when we said our vows six years ago. And the truth is, dear Meg, I do not think I love him any longer, either. It isn't only how much he has changed, his self-pity. I would not admit it to myself until lately, but we were growing apart even before the accident.

Yet I do not know if I have the courage to leave him, or even if leaving is the right thing to do. It might make things even worse for him. I feel as though I would be betraying him.

Rose blotted the last few words, reread all that she'd written, very nearly crumpled the paper. Her face felt hot, moist, and not only with the heat that lay thickly in the room. She dried her cheeks with her apron, tucked a damp wisp under the comb that held her fine brown hair in place. Outside, the two Bennett kids were bouncing a rubber ball off the wall of their house; the steady thump, thump, thump and their intermingled shouts and laughter echoed through the fading afternoon and made Rose's head ache.

She drew another sheet of paper in front of her and once again picked up the pen.

There is another thing on my mind I must tell you about, for it makes the situation even more complicated. I have feelings for another man. No, you mustn't think I've shamed myself with him. Nor has he made improper advances, though I am quite sure he has feelings for me, too. His name is Matt Kincaid. He owns a small ranch in the nearby hills, where he raises cattle to feed the mill workers.

The pen felt slick in her fingers; she laid it down. When she reread these last words, they struck her as foolish and awkward. How could she send this to Meg? She crumpled the sheet, stood, and put it on the dying embers inside the stove. Waited until it caught and flamed before she returned to the table.

Matt Kincaid remained in her thoughts, as he often did these days, and she felt guilty and selfish, as if by thinking about him she were indulging in a form of adultery. The rational part of her mind rejected that, but the emotional part would not release her from her commitment to Will. If their marriage was intolerable now, who was to say it wouldn't become better with the passage of time? If she felt a strong attraction to Matt Kincaid, who was to say it was not simply a passing fancy created by the events of the past six months?

She couldn't decide what was true and what was right. All she knew for certain was that she must make a decision one way or another, and that it must be made soon.

She also knew, now, that she couldn't tell Meg about Matt Kincaid, at least not yet. Nor, for that matter, about the extent of her troubles with Will. Meg would understand—but it was something she must work out alone, and it must not have anything to do with whether or not she decided to leave her husband.

Feeling very much alone, Rose took the first page of the letter and burned it, too, in the stove.

2

The Big Tree Saloon had been deserted except for Pete Weidenbeck, who ran it for Austin Trace, when Denbow got there and claimed the puncheon table by the front window. Then Sam Honeycutt and that rancher, Kincaid, had come in, and later Burt Eilers, and then a rough-dressed stranger who had the look of a teamster. Now, with the day shift at the mill ended, the place was packed tight. The poker and faro tables were open, and Ollie Kimbrough was playing his accordion, and there was plenty of laughter and good fellowship. Denbow preferred it this way, even though he was still alone at the table and didn't enter into any of the conversations. He had enough emptiness and silence at home; here there was a sense of kinship. They all pitied him, sure, just as Rose did, and he hated their pity and their pretense that nothing had changed. But that didn't stop *him* from pretending he still belonged.

Wasn't much, but it was all he had left.

He drank from his fifth glass of beer, stared out through the window at the mill compound. Twelve years, he thought. The only job he'd ever had except for the summers he'd spent with his old man working the switch engine in the Oakland yards. A friend of Pa's had gotten him on at the mill here. Yard laborer, helper of Ben Purdom's rail crew, then first assistant in no time. He'd have been made crew chief when Ben retired, no question of that, if it hadn't been for that damned day one of the hoist lines broke as they were loading cut logs onto a flatcar and a rolling log caught him and crushed his leg, crushed his future along with it.

Twelve years. He was a mill hand, a railroad worker; he didn't know how to do anything else, hadn't *wanted* to do anything else. Now he was nothing. Half a man, a cripple. Would have been better if that log had landed on his head instead, put him out of his misery right then and there.

Moodily he rolled and lit a cigarette. No damn good to himself anymore, and no damn good to Rose, either. Not that that didn't work two ways. Her always yapping about starting a new life, pretending like everybody else that things weren't as bad as they seemed. Harping at him, pitying him. Maybe it'd be best for both of them if she moved on back to San Francisco and left him to fend for himself. He'd find some way to survive. He didn't need her or anybody else.

Talk and laughter rose and fell around him, with Ollie Kimbrough's accordion music rolling out jauntily in the background. He was sealed off from it, but he listened, anyway. Sam Honeycutt holding forth about what it was like working for the U.P. in the "Hell on Wheels" days after the war. Joe Ashmead and Burt Eilers and Cletus Boone talking about the fire over at Pine Hill. Al Baker and Webb Murdock yakking about something funny that had happened at the mill today. Nobody saying anything about how bad things looked, not tonight for a change. That subject had been talked to death; there was nothing any of them could do except wait it out, see what Trace decided to do in the end. If somebody started in on it, the music and laughter would die and the rest of the evening would be like an Irish wake.

Denbow sat alone because he had nothing to say himself, on any subject. He'd tried joining in a couple of times, right after he'd recovered from the surgery, but it had been awkward and painful—everybody uncomfortable, talk drying up, pity beating at him in waves. So he'd given up, let them know he wanted nothing more from them than to sit alone in their midst.

He finished his beer, shifted around on the bench to wave his empty glass at Pete Weidenbeck behind the plank. Weidenbeck didn't see him at first; he was serving the rough-dressed stranger another full glass. Denbow shouted above the din, "I'm next, Pete." Weidenbeck heard that, nodded, and lifted his hand.

When Denbow swung back, he saw Kincaid get up from where he was sitting next to Honeycutt and make his way over. The rancher stopped in front of him, produced a smile, and said, "Evening, Will."

Denbow scowled at him.

"Thought you might like some company."

"Yeah? Well, you thought wrong."

". . . Buy you a beer?"

"I don't take handouts."

"I'm not offering one—"

"I'll pay for my own beer."

Kincaid kept standing there. His eyes were solemn—like Rose's eyes, like all their eyes when they looked at him. Big son of a bitch, quiet and easygoing, but tough in his own way. Even though he was an outsider, owned his piece of land just a year, the others liked him and accepted him. Denbow didn't like him at all. The pity was one reason, but the main one was that Kincaid was sniffing around Rose like a mongrel dog after a bitch in heat.

You'd have to be blind not to see it in the way he looked at her. And maybe she fancied him, too—likely did, judging from the one time he'd caught her looking back at Kincaid. Wasn't anything improper between them—Denbow would have known it if there was, for Rose could never lie to him— but there might be if he was out of the way.

"Well?" he said, sharp. "Why don't you drift?"

"All right," Kincaid said. "Sorry."

"Sorry? What the hell for?"

"Bothering you."

"Then quit doing it."

Kincaid shrugged, turned away. Denbow was aware that Honeycutt and Ashmead and a couple of the others were watching him; he glared at each of them until they shifted their gazes.

Weidenbeck came over with the fresh glass of beer. Denbow said, "Wait," and caught up the glass and drained it in a single convulsive swallow. He wiped his mouth, handed the empty glass back to Weidenbeck. "Again."

"Sure. Sure, Will."

Denbow looked out the window again. He had to relieve himself, but he'd wait until everybody went home to their wives and kids for supper. He'd wait all night if he had to. He wasn't going to let them see him get up and hobble out to the privy on his goddamn crutch.

3

They had made camp two-thirds of the way down the west slope, in a cleared area near where a logging track intersected the main road down into the valley. There was plenty of room for the Espenshied, a stream nearby, and enough grass for the oxen. The animals were still yoked and chained; Rudabaugh had wanted them kept that way, to save time if he decided to go after the munitions tonight.

And that was just what he *had* decided, after two hours of scouting and another hour of listening to talk in the Big Tree Saloon.

It was near dark when he got back to the camp. Patch and Chavis were eating hardtack and jerky and cold beans; he'd told them not to make a fire because he didn't want to call attention to them or to the big freighter. The oxen moved sluggishly in their traces, but the only sounds they made were the faint chink and jingle of their chains; Patch had removed the harness bells. The heat-heavy air was ripe with the stench of their droppings, and urine-damp.

Rudabaugh was hot and thirsty from the uphill climb. He went to the shallow stream first, filled his hat and doused water over his head, then drank out of his cupped hands. When he turned, he saw Patch and Chavis watching him. He went over and squatted next to Patch, who had his back up against one of the wagon's huge iron wheels, and stripped off a piece of jerky for himself.

"Anybody come by with questions?" He'd told them to say that they were freighters out of Ukiah, that they'd had to lay over here for repairs on the wagon.

Patch shook his head. Chavis said, "Only seen one man with a wagon, and he never give us a look. How's the lay down there?"

"Same as it looked from up above. Good."

"What about Trace?"

"He's here," Rudabaugh said. It was what he'd gone to the saloon to find out.

"So we do it tonight?"

"No sense in waiting."

Patch stirred himself. He had a twitchy look about him now, as if something had spooked him. "You *sure* Trace ain't got anybody in that house with him?"

"No family left, woman who cooks for him lives in town. I told you that already."

"Armed guards is what I meant," Patch said.

"I told you that, too. If he brought in guards, people would start getting curious. Nobody here knows what he's been up to."

"All seems too damn easy. . . ."

"Sure it is," Chavis said. He was rolling one of his loose, dribbly cigarettes. "You think we'd be here if it wasn't, just the three of us?"

Patch's eyes twitched between Chavis and Rudabaugh, then skyward, then back to Rudabaugh. "Mountain lumber mill," he said. "It's a hell of a place to cache weapons."

"Not when you look at it with Trace's eyes. Only better place would be a church."

"He must be crazy, this Trace. Buildin' an army and

cachin' weapons to wipe out a bunch of Indians. Craziest thing I ever heard.''

"Sure he's crazy," Rudabaugh agreed. "So what?"

"Can't tell what a crazy man will do, that's all."

Rudabaugh's patience was wearing thin. "You want shut of this, Patch?" he said, soft.

Patch scrubbed a hand through his whiskers. His eyes flicked skyward again, somewhere beyond Rudabaugh's left shoulder. "No," he said. "I come this far."

"What makes you so jumpy? You act like a horse with burrs under his blanket.''

"Nothing," Patch said. And once more his gaze went up and to the northeast.

This time Rudabaugh turned to see what Patch was looking at. The only thing in the night sky off that way was a faint smoky-red glow above the wooded hills. If you looked at it long enough, the glow seemed to pulse some.

"Forest fire," he said, and the words made Patch jump. "Place called Pine Hill. They were talking about it in the saloon.''

"How far away?" Patch asked nervously.

"Thirty miles. What the hell, Patch?''

"I don't like fires.''

"No? Why not?''

Patch grimaced and shook his head.

Chavis said, "Shit, man, it's thirty mile away. It ain't goin' to run on over here and roast *you*.''

"Shut up! Shut up about that!''

The sudden, sharp words surprised Rudabaugh. Most men were afraid of Chavis and spoke careful around him; until now Patch had been no exception. It was no surprise that Chavis didn't like it. He swung around to face Patch, his huge hands as big as the heads on a pair of nine-pound hammers.

"What the hell you say to me?''

"Just don't talk about roastin' nobody—''

Chavis hit him, a backhanded blow that knocked Patch over backward and bounced his head off one of the wagon's iron tires. Blood crawled out of Patch's mouth like shiny black snake; he lay there dazed. Chavis would have hit him again if Rudabaugh hadn't caught one of his arms and said, "Easy, Chavis, you want to lay him up so he can't drive the wagon?"

He had to say it again before the words cut through Chavis's anger, meant enough for the tightness in him to loosen. Chavis shrugged off his hand and said, "He talks to me like that again, I'll break his goddamn neck."

"All right."

"You hear me, Patch? I'll break your goddamn neck."

Patch made a sound in his throat but no words.

Rudabaugh said, "We got work to do. Chavis, climb inside and get the lantern ready. Don't light it yet."

Chavis hesitated, glaring down at Patch. Rudabaugh said, "Go on," keeping his voice neutral. Chavis moved then, around to the rear of the Espenshied, where he yanked aside the canvas draw curtain that hung from the wagon's tilt. He climbed up inside.

Rudabaugh watched Patch get slowly to his feet, spit out a glob of blood. He'd worked with all kinds of men over the years, hard and soft and everything in between; these two weren't the worst, but they weren't the best, either. He hadn't had any trouble with them coming up from San Francisco, and he'd better not have any more than this one little skirmish. Patch and Chavis weren't going to botch *this* job. He'd shoot both of them before he let that happen, even if it meant loading and driving the Espenshied himself. This was the biggest job he'd ever been a part of, and if it went according to plan, it would be his last.

More than a quarter of a century on the owlhoot trail— ever since those days back on the Kansas-Missouri border before the war, when he'd been a wild-ass button. Had his share of adventure and excitement in all that time; rode with Quantrill later on, among others, and killed his share of men, and felt the weight of thousands of dollars in his pockets more times than he could count. But the money hadn't stayed in his pockets long. No, it all went into the purses of deadfall owners and whores and faro bankers. Getting on in years now, forty-two his next birthday; grown tired of the fancy women and the company of men like Patch and Chavis, and of the fear of a hangrope that still ran so deep and raw in him that it troubled his sleep and woke him up sometimes, all fevered and shaking.

The West was changing, changing fast. Why couldn't he change with it? There was a roadhouse up at Whiskey Slough in the Sacramento Delta—run-down place that could be bought cheap. Buy it, fix it up, put in some gaming tables for the suckers, hire a couple of percentage girls . . . hell, he could live out his days in comfort and ease. That was just what he planned to do. And nobody, least of all a couple of rattlepates like Chavis and Patch, was going to keep him from doing it.

Right now he'd handle them easy and quiet, with words. But after they had the munitions . . . well, what he did then was up to them. He went over to Patch, put a hand on his shoulder, and said in a voice that wouldn't carry, "Don't rile Chavis like that again. I mean it, Morley. He'll kill you, just like he said. I won't be able to stop him."

"Crazy," Patch said. "Him and Austin Trace both."

"You say that a little louder, he'll kill you right now. You want him to have your share?"

"No."

"Then don't rile him. Do what I tell you, keep your mouth shut, and don't worry about a forest fire that's thirty miles away. We'll be back in San Francisco in three days, lying with twenty-dollar whores, before that fire ever gets anywhere close to this valley. Hear?"

"I hear."

"Go on into the wagon."

He gave Patch a little push, followed him around to the rear and up into the cavernous space—all of it empty except for Chavis and the few supplies they'd brought with them. Rudabaugh told Chavis to light the lantern. A sulfur match flared, filling the wagon with its fumes. While Chavis attended to the lantern, Rudabaugh took the map out of his shirt and spread it open on the rough bed boards.

The map had been drawn by a gent named Duggan in San Francisco who had once worked for the Big Tree Lumber

Company. Rudabaugh didn't know where Untermeyer had found Duggan; Untermeyer knew things the president of the United States didn't know and could find people the Secret Service couldn't. It was Untermeyer who had gotten wind of Austin Trace's cache of weapons, and Untermeyer who had hired Rudabaugh, and Untermeyer who would pay him thirty thousand in gold and Chavis and Patch each twenty thousand when the ordnance was delivered to him at his freight warehouse on the Embarcadero. What Untermeyer intended to do with the guns and ammunition, how much a profit *he* would realize, was nobody's business but Untermeyer's. All Rudabaugh cared about was his thirty thousand and the roadhouse it would buy him at Whiskey Slough.

He took the lantern from Chavis, set it down where the flickery light shone on the map. "All right," he said. "Now this is what we do . . ."

CHAPTER 3

1

MATT KINCAID'S RANCH WAS TUCKED INTO ONE CORNER of a little mountain valley two miles from Big Tree. One-room cabin, barn and corral, combination woodshed and icehouse—all of which he'd built himself, his first spring and summer here, keeping house in a tent until the cabin was finished. A creek came down out of the heights and meandered along the edge of the meadow where his cattle grazed. Good sweet grass, plenty of shelter from the winter snows, and only one narrow track in and out of the valley that he had fenced and gated to keep the cows from roaming. He had over thirty head of prime beef now, intended to run a peak number of eighty—about all the valley would support.

It was an easy life, a good life. Or it had been until he began to take notice of Rose Denbow. And until Austin Trace's odd behavior put the mill's future in jeopardy. Now nothing seemed simple or easy any longer.

Dusk was falling when he returned from Big Tree. The meadow grass was sun-dried from the long drought—more than three months now since the last rain—and he thought again of the fire over at Pine Hill. The faint glow of it was visible to the northeast, a ruddy, sullen stain on the gathering dark. The fire danger was just as bad here, as Sam Honeycutt had reminded him earlier: one more thing to fret his mind.

He took his grulla into the corral, unsaddled the animal, rubbed it down, then turned it out with his other horse, a

26

blaze-faced roan. Then he forked some hay into the trough for them. The sky was blue-dark by the time he finished, except for that stain in the direction of Pine Hill. He went into the cabin. Evening shadows and thick heat filled it; he set about lighting one of the lamps.

The furnishings—and his belongings—were few. This was because his needs were simple. Food, water, a comfortable chair, a comfortable bed, a book to read now and then: what else did a man need? Well, now there was a different answer to that question. And that answer made the cabin seem barren and wanting tonight.

The heat and the beer he'd drunk at the Big Tree Saloon had made him thirsty. He caught up the bucket and went out to the creek. Usually it ran full, even in the summer; now, after all the rainless days, it was less than half its normal size. But at least the water was still cold and sweet. He filled the bucket, took it back inside, drank two dippersful and part of a third before he had slaked his thirst.

Too hot to build a cookfire, he decided. He cut two thick slices off the loaf of bread he'd made from ground acorn meal and pine nuts, slathered butter on each, added two slices of cold beef. He'd thought he was hungry, but when he took a bite of the sandwich, he found that he wasn't. He forced himself to eat, anyway.

He thought again that he shouldn't have approached Will Denbow in the saloon. Denbow was Rose's husband, for one thing; and for another, he was a bitter, angry man who spurned everyone since the mill accident and the loss of his leg. So what was the sense in trying to hold a conversation with him? Kincaid had done it on impulse, without purpose . . . and yet it bothered him that he might have had a purpose after all. Such as wanting to convince himself that Denbow, in spite of his handicap, was unworthy of Rose. Such as looking for a convenient excuse to act on his own feelings for her.

He didn't want to believe he was that desperate. But maybe he was. He had never been in love before, had never had to cope with feelings as strong as this. He'd been a solitary boy, growing up in that orphans' home in Modesto, and he'd been a solitary man through the succession of jobs—farm worker, cowhand, mustanger—that had led him from the San Joaquin Valley to this mountain retreat. In the past he'd always shunned personal involvements as a threat to his freedom and his solitude; when the need for a woman became too strong, as it did once or twice a year, there were always bawdy houses nearby—one in Springwood that he'd visited last fall.

But now his freedom seemed empty, and the solitude had become something that approached loneliness.

He kept telling himself that he wasn't a wife stealer; that trying to take Rose away from a one-legged man wasn't just shameful, it was devilish. But all the inner talking hadn't done a lick of good. When it came right down to his own peace of mind, his own needs, he suspected he wasn't selfish enough or charitable enough to do the gentlemanly thing.

Sooner or later, right or wrong, he was going to force the issue with Rose.

And if she spurned him, as likely she would? Would he be strong enough then not to keep on pursuing her? He thought perhaps he would, but he didn't know for sure. He didn't want to think about it. This whole business was painful enough as it was.

Kincaid finished his sandwich, but only because he didn't believe in wasting food, and cleaned up after himself as he had been taught to do in the orphanage. When he was done, he stood in the middle of the room and looked at his books. No, there was no use in trying to read; he wouldn't be able to concentrate tonight. At length he lighted his big railroad lantern and carried it outside to the woodshed.

It was full dark now. There was starlight but no moon yet. The breeze of the afternoon had died and the air was hot, still, heavy with the scent of dry grass and resin. Insects buzzed and sang; there were rustlings in the woods beyond the creek. Another peaceful summer night.

Another lonely summer night.

Damn it, he thought. He got the double-bitted ax out of the shed, set to splitting logs into firewood for the coming winter. He worked fast and hard, swinging the ax almost savagely, until sweat drenched him and the muscles in his arms and shoulders began to ache.

But it was no use. No use at all.

At the end of an hour he put the ax away, went back into the cabin to sponge the sweat off his body, and put on a clean shirt and a clean pair of Levi's. Then he saddled the roan and rode out across the meadow and up through the cut and down into Big Tree Valley.

He was not going to see Rose; he was only taking a ride to relax him so he could sleep, going back into town for another beer at the saloon—where Will Denbow would still be sitting, as he sat every night until the midnight closing. He was not going to see Rose, not tonight, not yet.

Lying to himself all the way down.

2

Sitting on the porch, in the shadows cast by the old tan oak tree that grew beside the house, Rose saw the shape of a man come along the dusty street and pause outside the gate. At first she couldn't tell who it was; then, when he turned to the gate and opened it, she recognized him.

Matt Kincaid.

She felt surprise and puzzlement—and a faint quivering in her stomach, a tightening of body muscles. She watched him walk slowly up the path to the porch and mount the stairs. The shadows hid her from him, and he went ahead to the screen door. He hesitated again, seemed to take a breath, and finally reached out to knock.

Rose found her voice. "I'm over here."

His head swung toward her; then he moved over to where she sat. "I didn't see you in the dark," he said.

"I know."

"Too hot inside?"

She nodded. "It isn't much better out here."

There was an awkward silence, as if he didn't know what to say next. Or as if he knew exactly what he wanted to say and was reluctant to say it. Rose sensed that there was a tautness in him, an uncertain purpose, and she was suddenly afraid. Of his feelings for her. Of hearing them spoken, being confronted with them. And of herself because she was not ready to face any of it yet.

She said, "Why are you here?"

"I . . . think we should talk."

"It's late for a social call."

"I know. But we have to talk, Rose."

"Mrs. Denbow," she said, even though they had been on a first-name basis for some time. "What is it you want to talk about?"

"I think you know."

"No," she said. "No, I don't."

". . . May I sit down?"

No, she thought. And said, "Yes."

He sat on the chair beside her, not touching her, being very careful about that. It was difficult to tell in the darkness, but his face seemed full of conflict. *This isn't any easier for him than it is for me*, Rose thought. But she sensed that he would go ahead with it just the same. As if he were compelled—and that frightened her all the more.

He said, "What do you think of me?"

". . . I don't understand what you mean."

"How do you feel about me?"

"I have no feelings for you," she said quickly. "I hardly know you."

"You do have feelings. I think they're the same as mine for you."

"No," she said.

"Yes. Yes, Rose."

She sat stiffly, not responding.

"Rose?"

"I think you had best leave now," she said, but there was no forcefulness in the words. She folded her hands, held them tight together in her lap.

"Not until you tell me the truth."

He put out a hand, touched her arm. Even through the sleeve of her shirtwaist, the contact sent little tremors through her. She drew away—too quickly.

Matt withdrew his hand. "I have to know," he said. "I need some idea of where I stand with you—"

"No," she said.

"Rose . . ."

"No."

"You do care for me, don't you?"

"I am going inside now. It's late." She started to rise.

"I love you," he said, blurting the words like a schoolboy.

She closed her eyes, opened them again, and made it to her feet. Turned away from him and stared past the branches of the oak tree at the sky to the northeast. A faint reddish incandescence tinged the horizon in that direction, like the last lingering afterglow of a sunset. The forest fire at Pine Hill, she thought distractedly. Raging out of control, a wild-fire—like her own emotions at this moment.

Behind her, Matt said in a low, shaken voice, "I'm sorry, I am, but I had to say it. I had to get it into the open."

"I don't want to hear such words . . ."

"I love you," he said again.

"I'm married. You know that."

'Happily married?"

"Yes."

The lie seemed to hang in the dry, hot air.

"Look at me, Rose."

"No."

"Please look at me."

She didn't move.

He got to his feet. She heard him come up behind her, felt him standing there, and she tensed. But when he took hold of her arms, gently, and turned her toward him, the small tremors moved through her again. She wanted to draw away, as she had moments ago, only this time she could not make herself do it.

Her throat felt parched, her face hot and damp; she drew a breath, gathered herself, and lifted her head to look at him. Up close this way, the conflict in his face was more apparent. His eyes, dark-shadowed and steady, locked with hers, and she felt the yearning in them. They weakened her, stilled the lie she had been about to repeat.

"Rose?"

She heard herself say, "I don't know. I don't know. I need time to think."

"Then you do care for me."

"I don't know."

"All right. I won't bother you anymore—won't come here again. I'll abide by whatever you decide."

"Truly?"

"Yes. I won't shame you, Rose. I won't hurt you."

"You've already hurt me."

One side of his mouth twitched, as if with anguish. "I shouldn't have come, shouldn't have said . . . I know that. But I *had* to, I just . . . I couldn't stop myself."

From over at the Murdock house next door, a screen door banged and there was the sound of muted voices. Rose jerked her head around, stared over that way. Dear God, what if the Murdocks had overheard? Guilt welled up in her, made her back away from Matt until her hips came up against the porch railing. She listened, looking from the tree-shadowed front of the Murdock house and back to him again. Then, belatedly, she realized that the voices were coming from around back. Webb Murdock and his wife would have had to come slinking through the dark, spying, to overhear, and they weren't that sort at all.

"I'll go now," Matt said.

"Yes. Please go."

"Good night," he said gravely, and turned and left her alone.

She waited until he passed through the gate and started back toward Main Street. Then she sat down again in the shadows. In her mind she heard his voice saying the words that Will had not spoken to her in years, saying them over and over again like an echo that would not die: "I love you, I love you, I love you . . ."

Her hands were trembling.

3

Pete Weidenbeck leaned across the bar. "Closing up pretty soon, Will. You want one more?"

"No," Denbow said without turning his head.

"On the house . . ."

"I said no."

Denbow threw his last cigarette into the spittoon, pressed the heels of his hands to his temples. He'd had a dozen glasses of beer tonight and his stomach felt queasy and his head ached. But he wasn't drunk. Dull his mind, but he couldn't deaden it. Couldn't forget the accident, couldn't forget the stump or the crutch. Hell, just the opposite. The more he drank, the more he thought about them. When he was feeling his liquor, he could almost feel his right leg, too, little twinges in the knee, the ankle, the toes. Ghosts haunting his mind. Dead leg twitching in his memory.

He wondered what the Springwood doctor had done with the leg after he'd cut it off. Burned it? Buried it? Dead and gone, whatever—didn't exist any longer. Piece of him didn't exist any longer. Doc should have told him what he'd done with the leg. Man had a right to know where a piece of him went. Should have given the leg to him, for that matter. Man had a right to bury his own leg, didn't he?

Hell with it. Denbow scraped his chair back, caught his stump in both hands, and dragged the wooden leg out from under the table. Used the tabletop to lift himself upright. When he glanced toward the bar, Weidenbeck was washing glasses in the water tub with his head bowed and his eyes averted. Had to give him that much, Denbow thought bitterly. He knew better now than to gawk at a cripple.

Denbow hobbled over to the door and went outside. The street was empty, the dust on it settled for the night. Kids had been out there earlier, chasing each other, rolling hoops. They were worse than adults, the way they looked at him: cruelty mixed with pity, laughing at him behind their hands, making fun of him. Good thing he and Rose hadn't had any kids. Living with her was hard enough now; he'd go crazy if he had to put up with a kid all day long.

Some unsteady on his good leg, he made his way along Main Street. A breeze had come up, blowing down from the north, but it was hot and dry and did nothing much to ease the night's heat. If anything, it mixed with the beer he'd drunk to draw an oily sweat out of him. He could feel it trickling down his sides, chafing at his crotch.

When he came onto the side street where he lived, he saw two men standing at the gate of Sam Honeycutt's house—Honeycutt and Ben Purdom. They played cribbage most nights, but usually they were done by the time he came by. Now, sure as hell, they stopped talking and turned to look at him.

"Evening, Will," Honeycutt said.

"Evening."

Purdom said, "Hot night."

Denbow didn't bother to answer that. He started on past them.

Honeycutt said, "Hold on a second, son."

Damn. "What is it?"

"You give any more thought to my proposal?"

"No."

"I sure could use a helper in the yards. Lot of work to be done, and I been spendin' too much time on that Baldwin—"

"Sure you have. And a cripple's just what you need to ease your burden."

"You get around pretty good, seems to me."

"I'm not interested," Denbow said. "I told you that already. And even if I was, you think Trace would pay for the likes of me when he's already laid off better than two dozen able-bodied men?"

"We could work something out—"

"Yeah. Charity. I don't want your damn charity."

"I'm not offerin' charity, son. I'm offerin' you a chance to work. You know trains near as well as I do—"

"No," Denbow said. "How many times you want me to say it?" He swung away from them and stumped upstreet.

He could feel their eyes on him, hear the faint murmur of their voices. Talking about him behind his back, the way they always did. Poor Will Denbow, poor cripple, won't let no-body do anything for him. Why, how are he and his poor missus going to get along when their savings runs out? Bull-shit. Didn't understand him, none of them. Wouldn't leave him alone, neither. That was all he wanted, for Christ's sake, for them to leave him the hell *alone*.

Rose had left one lamp lit for him in the front room. Afraid he'd stumble in the dark, fall on his face. Like he'd done that afternoon. Light or dark, what difference did it make? He went to the lamp, not being quiet about it, and lifted the chimney and snuffed the flame. In the bedroom, enough moonlight filtered through the open window to show him Rose lying on her side of the bed. Only she wasn't asleep; hadn't been asleep, likely. He heard her stir, sit up as he undressed. Watching him. Always watching him.

"Will?"

"Go to sleep," he said.

"I can't sleep. I've been waiting for you."

"Start in about loving again, I suppose."

"No. Not unless it's what you want."

"Well, it isn't."

Denbow unbuckled his belt, dropped his Levi's, and stepped out of them clumsily. Went over to sit on the bed and unfasten the straps of his peg leg. He threw the leg on the floor; it made a sharp clattering noise as it struck one of the walls. Then he lay back with one arm over his eyes. Sleep commenced to move in on him right away.

Rose said, "Will, I need to talk . . ."

Ah, Christ! He rolled onto his side and put the pillow over his ears to shut out the sound of her voice.

CHAPTER 4

1

THEY MOVED OUT SOME PAST ELEVEN O'CLOCK.

There was a moon now, and it shed enough light for them to see the road clearly as they set out with the freighter. Patch drove slowly, to minimize the creak and rattle of the wagon, the thump of the iron tires, the jangle of the trace chains. The noise they did make wouldn't carry far, Rudabaugh thought. Down in the valley, only a few lights showed like little burning holes in the sultry dark. One of the lights was in the watchman's shack at the main entrance to the mill compound. Trees screened the rest of the compound until they got down near the western perimeter. Then Rudabaugh could see that there were lights in the big sawmill over at the east end—and no lights at all in Austin Trace's house at the near end.

The place he'd picked for Patch to wait with the Espenshied was a few hundred yards uphill from the mill's front gate, in another little clearing just off the road. Once they got into the clearing, the gate was partially obscured by trees. The high fence that enclosed the compound ran at a forty-five-degree angle to the road, through high brown grass and thick underbrush; forty yards of that rough, open ground separated the fence from the clearing. On the opposite side of the road, a densely forested slope hid the town in the shallow valley below. There were woods behind the clearing on this side, too, extending up around and behind the mill.

When Patch halted the team, Rudabaugh glanced sideways at him to see how he was holding up. Still twitchy; still glancing now and then at the fire glow in the distance. But there was no real daunciness in him. He would stand up to the waiting all right.

Rudabaugh swung down, waited for Chavis to come around from the other side. They were both wearing their revolvers now, holsters tied down. He'd had that .45 Colt of his twenty years; it was a better and more trustworthy friend than any man he'd ever known.

There was no need for talk; they had said all that needed to be said earlier, gone over everything again and again until even Chavis had it down right. Rudabaugh led him across the open ground to the fence, along the fence another fifty yards to the place he'd found during his scouting expedition that afternoon. One of the redwood fence sheets had warped away here, leaving a gap wide enough for a man to crawl through.

Once he was inside, Rudabaugh stayed down on one knee to study the compound. Not far away were a couple of long lean-to arrangements under which were ricks of board lumber, stacks of plywood, and redwood sheets. The sawmill bulked up well beyond, at the far side of the compound, shedding a broad shine of lamplight. The whine of the big steam saw came now, as it did at intervals. But there was only a skeleton crew working the night shift these days; he had confirmed that during his time in the Big Tree Saloon. That made things easier.

He felt Chavis, quiet as a cat for all his size, brush up alongside him. But his gaze shifted the other way, to where Austin Trace's house squatted on its rise of land. Big place, two-storied, built after the fashion of swells' houses in San Francisco. No light showed anywhere on either floor.

He nudged Chavis and then pushed up into a crouch and moved through the shadows to the closest of the lean-tos. Went along the rows of board lumber, past a second lean-to, across to where three conical mounds of sawdust loomed black against the moonlit sky. The smell of the sawdust was sharp in the air. Too sharp: it made you want to sneeze. Rudabaugh commenced breathing through his mouth.

They stopped behind one of the mounds, putting it between them and the sawmill. Forty yards to their left was the squat shed in which dynamite and black powder was kept for stump blasting and road building. Rail tracks ran past it on the far side; one of the wagon tracks that crisscrossed the compound paralleled the tracks. Beyond the powder shed was fifty yards of ground sloping up to where Trace's house sat. There was plenty of cover between the sawdust mounds and the powder shed—open ricks of beam lumber and redwood blocks—but those fifty yards had nothing on them except clusters of ferns and scrub brush. And the moon was bright now, bathing the slope in its milk-white shine.

Rudabaugh looked back behind them, to the northwest. Up there, the fence ran through a line of trees that hadn't been cleared off. Inside and outside the compound, the trees extended around behind Trace's house. There was still thirty yards or so of open ground between the woods and the house, on the west side and in back, but if they came in from the rear, they couldn't be seen by anybody at the gate or the sawmill.

Rudabaugh set off in a humped-over run away from the sawdust mounds to the powder shed; Chavis was right behind him. From there he could see part of the mill gate and all of the watchman's shack. The watchman's lantern was lit but there was no sign of the man himself.

With the powder shed at their backs they ran diagonally toward the fence, keeping to the shadows. They had to cross more open ground near the fence, so when they got up into the trees, Rudabaugh stopped to scan the compound again. But nobody had come out of the sawmill or the watchman's shack, and Trace's house was still dark and silent.

Quickly now, Rudabaugh led the way up through the trees. The closer they got to the house, the more carefully he watched where he stepped. Sounds carried on a hot night like this, and the ground was strewn with small dry branches and brittle twigs. When they reached a point opposite the rear corner, he halted again and gave the house a long look past low-hanging pine boughs. Two windows in the sidewall on the first floor, both of them shut. Across the rear was a veranda supported by latticed pillars; there were too many shadows for him to tell if any of the windows back there were open.

He moved out of the trees, Chavis following, across to where a set of stairs gave access to the veranda. They hunkered down there to listen. Silence from inside the house. Rudabaugh leaned up to peer at the windows: shut tight, all of them. He could go up there and check each one, but he didn't want to do that unless they were unable to find another way in. Old wood like those steps and the veranda floor was liable to creak loud as hell when you put your weight on it.

He motioned Chavis to stay where he was, took himself around to the west-side wall. At the nearest window he ran his fingers around the frame, squinted at the glass. There was a drawn curtain inside. He got a grip on the bottom of the sash and gave it just enough upward pressure to see if it would open. It wouldn't; locked or stuck tight. He moved to the second window, tugged up on its sash in the same way, with the same results.

When he came back around the corner, he shook his head at Chavis and moved on past to the east corner. The sawmill was visible from there, but the gate and the watchman's shack were obscured by a long tin-roofed train shed. Still nobody moving around down there. He eased along the wall to the first window on that side, tested it, found it locked or stuck like the others. Same thing with the next in line.

The third window, nearest the front, was open by a couple of inches.

Rudabaugh hooked his hands under the sash, lifted. It slid up a few more inches, soundlessly. The curtain inside billowed a little in the warm night breeze, but also without sound. He stepped away, went back around to where he could see Chavis, and waved for him to come ahead.

At the open window, Rudabaugh eased the sash up as far as it would go. The window was set low enough to the ground so that he had no trouble swinging a leg up and over the sill.

He pushed the curtain aside and lifted himself through the opening.

The room he was in seemed to be a study. He could make out the black shapes of a desk, a sofa, a couple of chairs. The door on the far side of the room was closed.

He beckoned to Chavis, who straddled the sill, got his broad back under the sash. But when he started to raise up inside, his shoulder caught the sash's bottom edge. The window rattled—not loud, but loud enough to freeze both of them where they stood.

Rudabaugh listened.

Stillness.

He waited a full minute before he moved again. He gripped Chavis's arm, hard, to tell him to watch what the hell he was doing. Chavis didn't object; he came in the rest of the way without disturbing the night-hush.

There was just enough in-spill of moonlight to show Rudabaugh an unobstructed path across to the door. Otherwise he would have had to strike a lucifer and he hadn't wanted to do that, more because of the sharp smell than the flare of light. He eased ahead across the carpeted floor, heel and toe. At the door he opened it a few inches and peered through the crack.

Hallway. He widened the opening, stepped through, padded down the hall to where it opened into a foyer with a staircase on the far side. He went to the foot of the stairs. He could hear the ticking of a clock somewhere; that was the only sound. When he looked up at the second-floor landing, he could just make out two closed doors, one on either side.

Slowly, Chavis at his heels, he began to climb.

2

Austin Trace slept lightly enough so that the opening of the bedroom door roused him. But it was one of two figures bumping against the canopied bed that brought him fully awake. He sat bolt upright, blinking in confusion. In the next second a hand clutched at his throat, drove him back hard against his pillows. Something cold and metallic jabbed against his right ear; then he heard the sharp and unmistakable click of a handgun's hammer being cocked.

"Don't struggle, old man," an unfamiliar voice said out of the darkness. "Don't move a peg."

Trace lay still. There was outrage building in him now, like a fire burning away the confusion. "Who are you?" he demanded. "What are you doing in my house? You have no right—"

"Shut up," the voice said. "No talk, no sass, just do what you're told and you'll live to see sunrise."

"What do you want?"

The voice said, "Find the lamp and light it," but it was not addressing him this time. Trace watched the other dark shape move around the bed, locate the lamp on his bedside table; heard the scrape of a match. He blinked at the bright flare, blinked again when the lamp's wick ignited and a dull yellow glow spread through the room.

He stared at the man holding the lamp, then shifted his eyes without turning his head to peer at the one pressing the revolver against his head. Strangers. Rough-garbed, hatless. One big, stupid-looking, with mean little eyes; the other just as tall but thinner, flecks of gray in his hair and mustache and the light of intelligence in eyes the color of suet pudding.

Dry-throated, he asked again, "What do you want?"

"First thing we want," the man with the gun said, "is for you to get out of bed."

"I don't—"

"No arguments. Out of bed."

Trace hesitated, but when the revolver jabbed his ear, he threw back the counterpane. In slow movements he swung his legs off the bed, stood up.

"Now get dressed."

Trace stepped sideways to the chair on which he had laid out his clothing, picked up his trousers, and began to put them on over his nightshirt. He was damned if he would strip naked before these two. He turned sideways to button his fly, then shrugged into his shirt.

He said, "I keep no money in the house, if that is what you're after. And I have no other valuables."

"Sure you do," the stupid-looking one said.

"I don't know what you mean."

"You got valuables, all right. A whole big storage shed full of valuables."

The munitions! They were after the munitions!

Understanding brought fear to him for the first time. Not for himself—he had never been afraid for his own life. Fear for his plan, his army of vengeance. How could these men have found out? The agents in San Francisco and Stockton who had sold him the weapons and ammunition? Damn their eyes!

His rage turned cold and calculating. He must not let them get away with stealing the ordnance. It was of no matter, really, who they were or how they had found out; all that mattered was that they must be thwarted at all costs.

A whole big storage shed full of valuables.

His mind worked rapidly. They seemed to know he had kept the munitions here in the compound—but did they know or suspect that he had had everything loaded into the two boxcars two nights ago? No. If they had known or suspected it, they would not have bothered to come here after him; they would have gone directly to the siding in town. The shipment *was* safe, then. There was nothing they could do to make him tell about the boxcars; he would die first, and gladly, if it meant that the ordnance reached Portland.

He finished dressing, slid his bare feet into his high-top shoes and squatted to tie the laces. When he straightened again, the thinner one said, "Downstairs. Step lively."

Trace walked out of the room in stiff strides. The two thieves followed close behind, the stupid-looking one bringing the lamp. On the lower floor they directed him into the study. They seemed to know where it was, and when he entered, he saw why. This was how they had gotten in; the front window was wide open.

The thinner one, the leader, gestured toward the desk. "Sit down. Fold your hands where I can see them."

Trace did that. When the stupid one put the lamp down next to him, its light glinted off the silver-framed photographs of Stephen and Clara. *I won't let them stop me*, he promised Stephen silently. *You mustn't fear, son. I'll find a way.*

The leader opened drawers to check for weapons, but there were none for him to find. Then he said, "All right. Take a sheet of paper and your pen and write what I tell you." He waited until Trace had pen in hand. Then he asked abruptly, "What's your night watchman's name?"

"Henry. Henry Judson."

"No it isn't. His name is Frank Bixby. You see, Trace? Tricks won't work with us. You just do as you're told and do it proper. Understood?"

"Yes."

"Write this to Bixby: 'Allow bearer of this note to pass through without question. He is delivering personal goods.' Then sign it."

"Bixby won't honor such a request."

"He'll honor it. Men here do what you tell them. Sign the note."

The thought was in Trace's mind to alter his signature, as a warning to Bixby. But these men seemed to know a great deal about him; it was likely they knew his signature as well. He signed in his usual hand, blotted the paper, and sat back.

The leader came forward to read what he had written. Then, with his free hand, he caught up the paper and passed it over to the stupid one. "Move out," he said. "Mind you're not seen."

"Don't worry about that." The stupid one climbed through the window and was gone.

Trace asked the leader, "What now?"

"Now we wait."

3

It took Chavis fifteen minutes to deliver the note to Patch. The waiting wasn't bad; everything was under control. Trace sat at his desk, hands folded, not saying anything, not even looking in Rudabaugh's direction. But Rudabaugh, leaning against the wall near the window, didn't take his eyes off the

mill owner. There was plenty of sly cunning in that old
booger. He had to know by now what they were after, and if
he was crazy enough to build an army to wipe out a bunch
of Indians, he was crazy enough to try something to save his
cache of weapons.

The house was quiet, except for the faint ticking of the
clock. Quiet outside, too—until boards creaked toward the
rear. Rudabaugh shoved away from the wall, shifting his
gaze between Trace and the window. Then Chavis's voice
said, "I'm back," and Rudabaugh relaxed.

"Any trouble?"

"No."

"Stay there. We're coming out."

He waggled his Colt at Trace, who got up out of his chair
and crossed slowly to the window. When they were both
outside, Rudabaugh said to him, "You lead the way. Don't
make any noise."

"Where?"

"You know where. Move."

Trace moved. Performed an almost military right-face and
headed for the east corner. Rudabaugh and Chavis followed
by a couple of steps, flanking him, both with their revolvers
at the ready. They went around the corner and along the
sidewall. Rudabaugh scanned the compound left to right,
right to left, but there was still nothing to see except moonlight and shadow and the fixed shapes spread throughout the
enclosure.

The storage shed—tin-roofed, with plank walls, built lower
to the ground than a barn and about half the size—was
seventy-five yards away, set at an angle between the house
and a couple of big kilns. One of the mill roads led up in
front of the shed, and a rail spur looped around to parallel
the south wall, ending at a right angle to the road. In the near
wall, facing west, was a set of tall double doors. There
weren't any windows that Rudabaugh could see.

Trace started straight down across the open ground. Rudabaugh stepped up to him quickly and cuffed his arm and
said, "Off to your left; keep the shed in front of you." No

argument. Trace changed direction immediately, led them due east, and then across the road above where the shed was.

They went down to the building, into the shadows along the west wall. When they came up to the double doors, Rudabaugh saw that they were fastened in the center by a padlock drawn through iron hasps. They would open outward and swing back against the wall, and the Espenshied could be backed off the road and right up to them for easy loading.

Without being told, Trace took a ring of keys from his coat pocket, picked out and opened the padlock. Left it hanging from one of the hasps and started to pull the doors open.

"I'll do it," Rudabaugh said. "You just back up out of the way."

Trace obeyed. Rudabaugh tugged the doors open. The hinges squeaked a little as the two halves fanned out on either side of him, but that kind of noise meant nothing now. He looked inside, couldn't make out much of anything in the blackness; he went ahead into the hot, stuffy interior by several paces. No need to worry about showing light now, either, not in here. He fetched out a lucifer, snapped it alight on his thumbnail.

The shed was empty.

Surprise and sudden anger prodded him into a fast turn. In that same instant he heard Chavis give a low cry—and then one of the door halves came flying inward, driving Chavis ahead of it.

Rudabaugh dropped the match. In the darkness Chavis was cursing and bulling around, and when Rudabaugh tried to run out through the open door, he banged into the careless son of a bitch and almost fell. Savagely he shoved Chavis out of the way, kicked the door wide, and stumbled outside again with his Colt up.

Trace wasn't there.

Trace was just disappearing around the far corner.

CHAPTER 5

1

By THE TIME RUDABAUGH GOT TO THE CORNER, TRACE was already on the far side of the rail spur, thirty yards distant. He was heading south, away from the kilns toward a wagon road that ran straight to the sawmill.

Chavis came running up, carrying his revolver out in front of his body as if he were thinking about using it. Rudabaugh knocked the muzzle down with his left forearm. "No shooting, no shooting! Cut him off before he gets to the sawmill!"

Rudabaugh veered off at a sharp angle to his left. Looked back after several strides and saw that Chavis was running at an angle the other way. At least he had that much sense, damn his black soul.

Just before Trace got to the road, he threw a backward look of his own; saw his pursuit and seemed to realize right away that he couldn't reach the sawmill before they reached him. Rudabaugh thought the crazy old booger would start yelling, knew if that happened he'd have to shoot him to save his own skin. But Trace didn't make a sound. And he didn't keep on going toward the sawmill. Instead he cut back to the west, across the road, plunged around one of the ricks of beam lumber, and vanished.

Rudabaugh could see the sawmill as he ran; there was still no sign of anybody out and about. He stared ahead at the rows of lumber. When he reached the road, he pulled up on the west side of it, in the shadows, and stood listening. From over west he heard faint scuffling sounds; then the sounds stopped and the night was quiet except for the muffled rasp of his breathing.

Chavis came up beside him. Rudabaugh said between clamped teeth, "Go down the rows, try to flush him out. I'll go around this end, make sure he doesn't double back."

"Yeah."

'Remember—no shooting."

"Yeah," Chavis said. He slid forward between two of the ricks and was gone.

Rudabaugh went the other way, around to the short section of open ground separating the beam lumber from the stacks of redwood blocks. The stacks were a good twenty yards wide and maybe seventy-five yards long, with narrow walkways between rows. Beyond were more open ground and the mounds of sawdust they had passed on their way in. Trace wasn't going to be able to come back this way, not without Rudabaugh spotting him. He had boxed himself into this part of the compound.

Moving in a crouch, Rudabaugh made his way forward.

2

Trace came out of the lumber to the west, paused there with his back up against the blunt end of a beam. The road nearby was deserted; so was the section beyond. Behind him, he could hear at least one of the thieves blundering around—not too close yet.

His pulse hammered in his ears; his face and hands were damp with sweat. But he was not afraid. Even now he was not the slightest bit afraid. What he felt was a kind of desperate excitement—the same sort of excitement he had anticipated feeling when he came face-to-face with Chief Joseph and smote him dead.

During his flight he had thought of shouting for help. But what could his unarmed employees do against these hard cases? And what if they found out about the ordnance? No, it was him against the two thieves, his wit against theirs. He had gotten away from them at the shed and he would get away from them now, too. Or kill them if he had the chance. But at all costs save himself. He was the general and the paymaster: His army of vengeance would disintegrate without him to lead it, and his plan to obliterate the Nez Perce would die if he did. He was a practical man; he knew this as well as he knew his own mind.

He listened again, and again heard the movement in the ricks of lumber behind him, coming closer now to the end of one row. He couldn't stay here any longer. Make for the lean-tos to the south? Or for the powder shed to the north and then up into the trees above—

The powder shed!

Dynamite, black powder—weapons far deadlier and more threatening than a pair of handguns.

A new feeling surged through him, one of raw power and invincibility. The Angel of Death must feel like this, he thought. He took another look behind him at the lumber. And then made his run for the powder shed.

3

When Chavis couldn't find Trace anywhere among the lumber, he cut around one of the ricks and went back out toward the road. And there the old bugger was, running toward that squat building across the way.

Chavis stepped back into the shadows and watched Trace get to the building, duck out of sight around to the other side. No time to fetch Rudabaugh; he didn't need Rudabaugh to give him any more orders. He ran away from the lumber, straight across the road, and came in on the building to the west. There was no sign of Trace in the darkness here, or on the open ground beyond; he was still somewhere on the other side. Slowing, Chavis advanced along the sidewall.

He heard Trace before he saw him again. There were footfalls at the front wall, other sounds that Chavis couldn't identify. He bulled ahead, out to where he could see along that side.

A door to the building stood open, its padlock hanging from one hasp. Trace was inside, doing something inside.

Chavis couldn't see him clearly, just movement in the shadows. He went closer to the door, stood with his feet planted wide and his revolver at arm's length.

"Come on out of there, Trace."

The sounds inside quit. There was a silence before Trace said, "No. Stand back, I warn you."

"You ain't warnin' nobody. Come out or I'll come in and drag you out."

"I have five sticks of dynamite in my hand. All capped, with short fuses. I also have a match ready to strike."

Chavis felt a moment of confusion. Then he said "Bullshit."

"I am not bluffing."

"Bullshit," Chavis said again. "Where's all them weapons? What'd you do with 'em?"

"Gone. Shipped out two days ago."

"Where?"

"Where you'll never find them."

"You tell me where or you'll die screamin' for mercy." Chavis took a step forward and to his left, toward the open door.

"Stop! I mean it, I'll blow you to kingdom come."

He could see Trace better now, the shape of him there in the gloom. Didn't look like he had nothing in his hands. Powder shed? The hell it was! He couldn't remember Rudabaugh saying nothing about no powder shed.

"You ain't gonna blow nobody up," he said, and flung himself through the doorway.

His shoulder made meaty contact with some part of Trace's body, brought a grunt, and staggered both of them. One of Chavis's legs got tangled up with Trace's; they went down together, thudding against a heavy keg or hogshead. Chavis tried to use his Colt as a club but the old bastard clawed at his hand, managed to take a partial grip on the gun. Chavis was in a fury now. He tried to wrench the Colt away, flailing blindly with his free hand. But when he did that, Trace's grip tightened his finger on the trigger. Goddamn gun was going to fire—

That was his last thought, the last moment of his life.

When the gun went off, Chavis and Trace and the shed all erupted together in a great mushrooming explosion of heat and sound and flame.

4

The blast knocked Rudabaugh off his feet, rolled him over half a dozen times on the dusty roadbed.

He had just come out from the lumber, was starting across toward the powder shed. And the next thing he knew, he was picking himself up, dazed and bruised, and all around him was roaring fire and heat. Where the squat building had been was an inferno of belching flame and huge clouds of black smoke that turned the night sky as bright as noon. Sparks and spears of fire fell everywhere, dry grass was burning everywhere; tree boughs were blazing seventy yards off, by the west fence; the sawdust mounds were yellow-orange pyres; the board lumber and redwood blocks, strewn together now like the rubble of collapsed houses, were just starting to burn.

Rudabaugh staggered backward, one hand up to shield his face against the waves of superheated air. It seared his skin; the stench of burned hair and smoldering cloth made him gag. He was aware of stinging pain on his arms and legs, on his chest, and when he looked down at himself, he saw that cinders had opened widening holes in his clothing. He slapped at the holes, realized then that he had somehow managed to hang on to his Colt. Without thinking about it, he pouched the weapon.

Behind him, over the crackling noise of the fire, he could hear men shouting in confusion and alarm—the night crew at the sawmill. He swung his head from side to side, still backing away. Patches of fire everywhere he looked, rushing together in spots to form flaming barriers. No way to get out of the compound now except through the front gate.

He spun on his heel and ran.

CHAPTER 6

1

Kincaid WAS ON HIS WAY UP THE EAST TRAIL FROM TOWN, finally taking himself home after hours of pointless wandering. Ever since leaving Rose, he had ridden from one end of the valley to the other—a fool's ride, fueled by restlessness and a disinclination to return to his empty cabin. Sitting alone up there, hemmed in by four walls and loneliness, was far worse than being adrift under the open sky.

He was trying again to convince himself that he had done the right thing in declaring his love, when the night erupted with such force that the ground shook and the concussion almost pitched him out of the saddle.

The roan whickered in terror, reared, and buck-jumped; Kincaid fought to say on, managed to settle the horse enough so that he could rein it around. In disbelief he stared at the flame and smoke soaring skyward from inside the mill compound.

Sweet Jesus!

He put the skittish roan into a run back down the road, cut across toward the wide-open mill gate. Inside, shouting men were streaming toward it from the sawmill. Drawn up just outside was the big freight wagon Kincaid had noticed a few minutes earlier on his way past; it had just been turning onto the mill's access track, a curious sight at this late hour. Its six-yoke of oxen were pawing in the traces, bawling their heads off. The teamster wasn't even trying to hold them; he

51

stood off to one side—a heavyset, bearded man—and gawked at the flames with a slack-jawed fixity, as if he'd been enthralled by them. His face, under a black cap, glistened with sweat, and the reflected firelight made his eyes seem huge, glassy.

Kincaid dismounted and ran past the man and the bawling oxen, dodged through the outpouring of mill workers to the watchman's shack inside. From there he could tell that the main source of the blaze was some sort of shed across the compound . . . Christ, the powder shed? And he could see that the entire west side was rapidly sheeting with flame. Fire raced through the trees around Austin Trace's house, had already torched its roof and another shed farther east, was jacketing the kilns and making them glow a hellish cherry red.

The last of the mill hands ran toward him, and he recognized Jack Bennett, the foreman of the night crew. Kincaid shouted, "Jack, what happened?"

Bennett slowed. "Don't know. We were all working inside—"

The rest of his words were lost in the roar of another, smaller explosion muffled somewhat by the thrumming of the fire. A gout of flame and gray-black smoke burst upward a few hundred yards across the compound.

"Coal-oil tank!" Bennett shouted. "We got to get out of here, we don't have much time!" He rushed ahead to the gate.

Kincaid started to follow, held up when something over by the tin-roofed train shed caught his attention. He wheeled that way, squinting—and saw that it was a man running in awkward strides, outlined blackly against the high, shimmering glare.

Kincaid raced over to help him, thinking that it must be Austin Trace. The air was furnace-hot now, and the billowing smoke made it difficult for him to breathe. He held one arm crooked in front of his eyes to protect them. When he was twenty yards from the running man, he saw that it wasn't Trace after all, that it was a lean stranger dressed in the same dark clothing as the teamster outside. Cinders smoldered on his shirt and trousers; most of his hair had been singed off. He was gasping, choking on smoke. Tear streams made glistening patterns on cheeks flushed brick-red by the heat.

He didn't seem to see Kincaid, nearly collided with him. Kincaid sidestepped, got a grip on the man's arm to steady him; he could smell the sickening, pungent odor of scorched hair and flesh. For a second the stranger fought him in a panicky way, trying to pull free, but when Kincaid said in urgent tones, "Easy, mister, I'll help you out," the man blinked, focused on him, and stopped his struggles. Together, they plunged ahead for the gate.

The stranger stumbled twice but Kincaid still had hold of his arm, kept him from falling. They skirted the watchman's shack, went through the gate. The teamster was still there, staring at the fire, but now the big freight wagon was gone; Kincaid saw it lying broken on its side a short way up the east road, where the spooked oxen had overturned it. His roan was gone, too, likely chasing its own terror back to the ranch.

With the stranger in tow, he pounded away from the gate in the wake of the running mill hands. When he glanced back, he saw that the fire was feeding itself now on the walls and roof of the sawmill.

2

The explosion wrenched Denbow up out of sleep and into a half-sitting, half-crouching position on the bed. His heart raced wildly, his head throbbed with hangover and the heaving return to consciousness. He shook himself, listened. Quiet again. But too quiet, as if there were more sounds he was unable to hear yet.

Outside the southwest window, the sky was tinged with a suggestion of flickering reddish light.

Beside him, Rose said, "My God, what was that? It sounded like—"

"An explosion, yeah."

"The mill?"

"Go outside and look."

She swung out of bed immediately, caught up her robe, pulled it over her shoulders as she hurried out. Denbow pressed his hands to his temples, dragged them down over his stubbled cheeks. Grimaced at the sour aftertaste of the beer he'd drunk and stared at the faint, shimmery light beyond the window. Fire?

Fire?

He was fully awake then. He pushed himself off the bed. Doors had begun to slam in neighboring houses and there was the muted babble of voices raised in alarm. Enough moonlight came through the window to let him see his wooden leg lying against one wall, where he had hurled it earlier. He hopped over there, caught up the contraption, hopped back to the bed again.

He was buckling the harness when Rose came rushing back in. "Will, It *is* the mill—it's on fire! *The whole mill!*"

"Throw me my clothes. Hurry up!"

When he had his pants buttoned and his shirt on, he hobbled past Rose, who was still struggling into her own clothing, and on outside. At the foot of the porch steps he stood staring toward the mill. A pall of twisting black smoke obliterated most of the sky in that direction; below it, where the mill buildings stood, firelight stained the night a ruddy orange. The whole mill was afire, all right—but that wasn't all. The woods on the northwestern slope were flaming, too, the blaze feeding on dry needles and pitch-heavy wood.

God, he thought in awe, *it'll wipe out the town, the valley, everything*.

He propelled himself ahead to the gate, yanked it open. The streets had come alive with men, women, and children, running alone and in groups. One man had managed to get his buckboard hitched, but he was having a time holding his horse; the commotion and the smell of fire had frightened it. The panic would get worse, Denbow knew, for people and animals both. The thought was in everyone's mind that they had to get out of the valley before the fire spread and blocked off the two main roads. Urgency and fear were as palpable in the air as the sharp, wind-carried smell of smoke.

The screen door banged behind Denbow as he stepped out

to the edge of the road. Rose came running to join him, said something he couldn't hear over the racket. He wasn't paying her much mind, anyway; his attention was on the fire.

It was spreading with incredible speed, aided by gusts of the thin night breeze. Firebrands leapt from treetop to treetop on the slope above the mill, igniting pine and spruce needles in bursts of roiling flame. Fountains of sparks fanned up and out against the backdrop of smoke, showered down like a grotesque fireworks show.

There was no bitterness in him now, no feeling of emptiness or uncaring. For the first time since his accident he was facing a tragedy far greater than the loss of his leg, and it was having a profound effect on him.

It was making him care again.

3

Beside the Espenshied, Morley Patch stood in thrall of the fire raging across the compound. Part of his mind was aware of where he was and what he was seeing and hearing—men rushing past him, shouts, the clouds of smoke and the moaning whisper of the flames—but another part of his mind had turned inward, opened his memory so that he was also staring with horror at that other fire long ago, seeing it through ten-year-old eyes and hearing again the dying screams of his father.

Big man, his father, quick-tempered, drank too much and whored around, but still his father, still the man his mother loved. Running away from the burning barn that last night with the fire eating at his clothes and his flesh—horse kicked a lantern into him, that was what they said later must have happened—while he beat madly at the flames. And his mother shrieking, himself crying, helpless, watching his father run on fire and then fall into the barnyard and writhe around on the ground, screaming, "Help me, help me!" Racing over there with his mother to try to put him out, trying to put his father out like you would a burning torch . . . too late. Too late. And then seeing him charred and dead there in the yard, little wisps of smoke curling up, and hearing his mother say,

"Don't look, Morley, don't look," and having his head pulled around and held tight against her breast.

He'd been terrified that night and he was terrified now.

Someone came up close beside him. "Come on," a voice said, "get away from here, for God's sake!"

Patch just stood there.

"Come *on*, mister! What's the matter with you?"

He couldn't move, couldn't speak. The flames held him like the devil's own hand.

Fingers gripped his arms; he felt himself being turned away and half dragged down the road. He didn't struggle, but his head kept snapping around because the fire was a magnet for his eyes. He watched it all the way down the track and across the joining of the two main roads and onto the grassy flat beyond.

The human hands released him there and the man who had helped him kept on running. But Patch stood again as he had by the gate: rigid, staring. Dimly he heard more shouting, the bawling of kids and animals. Saw, at the edge of his vision, two more men run out of the mill gate and come toward him on the road.

Inside his head, his father screamed and screamed.

When the last two men reached him, he realized that one of them was Clee Rudabaugh. Most of Rudabaugh's hair had been burned off; his face looked burned and there were scorched holes in his clothes. Fire had almost got him, almost done to him what it had to Patch's father.

The other man looked at Patch and then said to Rudabaugh, "You be okay now?"

"I'll manage."

"What about you?" the man asked Patch. "You all right?"

A craziness was inside him now. Words came out of his throat in a thick rush: "I ain't gonna die the way he did."

"The way who did?"

"All in flames," Patch said. "Screamin'." He swung around, looked into town. "Get out of here, get away from the fire!"

Rudabaugh said, "Chrissake, Patch, what's the matter with—"

But Patch was already running for the intersection.

4

Kincaid took out after the heavyset teamster, Patch, the other stranger running beside him. The entire mill was blazing now, and the fire had overrun its eastern boundaries; the high timberland to the northwest, north, and northeast was coated with capering flames that cast weird, shifting patterns across the sky. Smoke partially obliterated the west road and was beginning to undulate across the east road as well.

Any second now it'll jump both of them.

The thought put fear-cold on Kincaid's neck. He swiveled his gaze to the town; saw people and a couple of conveyances swarming onto Main Street, heading this way. All of them and all the buildings had a glazed look in the flickering reddish light: unreal, monstrous.

He looked over at the west road again, just as a firebrand hurtled out of the blaze on the northwest side, across the road. One of the trees there flashed with sudden fire that flung twigs and branches straight up into the air, consumed them before they could fall. A second later that tree became a black, smoldering skeleton while the fire raced on to the ones surrounding it.

Ahead, the heavyset teamster reached the intersection, tried to launch himself aboard an already packed spring wagon. Some hands sought to help him; others pushed him away. By the time Kincaid got to the wagon, the west road was shrouded in smoke and walled on both sides of crackling flames. And when he swung around, he saw the same thing happening to the east road.

Patch was clawing at the driver of the spring wagon, trying to take the reins from him; the driver struggled with him and his panicked horse, and was losing to both. Kincaid got a grip on the back of Patch's shirt, heaved him backward off the wagon, and wrapped his long arms around him. Patch struggled frantically, mewling; the lunging of his body staggered Kincaid. He tightened his hold, managed to get his legs braced wide apart, and the straining teamster jammed backward against his left knee.

The other stranger helped him by catching the front of Patch's shirt and slapping him sharply across the face with his other hand. "Snap out of it, Patch, goddamn you!"

Patch quit struggling; his muscles stiffened, then relaxed. He was breathing hard through his nose and mouth, still making those mewling sounds. When Kincaid eased his hold, Patch no longer tried to pull away. Kincaid let him go, stepped back. Patch stood still now, looking at the fire; he seemed to be transfixed again.

The townspeople were no longer swarming in this direction. The smoke and the fire's nearness had stopped them, frozen them for a few seconds. Their faces had an unnatural look in the firelight—twisted and shapeless with fear, like mummers' masks stained red-orange and sooty black.

Rose, Kincaid thought.

He looked for her, couldn't find her in the ragged mass of humanity. A feeling of desperate helplessness came over him. He wheeled around again to face the fire.

Flame swept across the tops of the trees from northwest to northeast. Less than three hundred yards upslope, both roads were invisible beneath dense coagulations of smoke. Growing wider and hungrier by the second, the blaze was already spread out before them like a gigantic wall a thousand yards long.

Wildfire.

And both roads to safety impassably blocked . . .

CHAPTER 7

1

ANY SECOND NOW THERE WAS GOING TO BE MASS PANIC.

Sam Honeycutt could see it in the faces of the men and women around him, hear it in their shrill voices and in the cries of the children. Feel it clogging the air as thickly as the scorching firewind and the choking smoke. And if it were allowed to ignite, it would spread with the same destructive speed of the fire.

Trapped, we're trapped!

No, he thought, no, by God, we're not!

He stepped quickly away from his wife, cupped his hands to his mouth to make himself heard above the crackling roar. "Listen, all of you!" he bellowed. "Listen to me! There's still a way out! By rail—we can get out by rail!"

For a moment it seemed that none of them comprehended what he was saying. Confusion and mounting panic still had control of them.

"I've got the Baldwin runnin' again!" Honeycutt shouted. "We'll couple it on to the passenger coaches, we'll outrun the fire to Springwood!"

The sense of the words finally got through to them. Heads and bodies had turned in his direction; there was a rising babble of voices. And the panic shattered like glass, and the shards were swept away in a surge of desperate hope.

"To the yards! Run for the yards!"

In a body, men and women scooping up the younger children, they rushed headlong back down Main Street. In their midst, Honeycutt watched the fire rage along the ridge to the northeast, beyond the siding where the coaches were. Blocks of flame streaked through the treetops, fragmented, and erupted forward like howitzer shells that landed fifty, a hundred yards ahead of the main blaze and exploded everything they touched. But there were better than three hundred yards of open ground between the fire's perimeter and the coaches, nearly all of it hard-packed dry earth that was grassless and treeless. Nothing much there for the blaze to feed on—unless a firebrand hurtled out and scored a direct hit on one of the cars.

When he came past the livery stable at the end of Main, Honeycutt veered over past the platform and work building to where the Baldwin sat under the water tower. A ragged group of others followed him. He brought his breathing under control, began barking out the names of men who worked on the rail crews at the mill.

"Purdom, Ashmead, Kimbrough, Murdock! You stay with me. The rest of you move on south, spread out along the tracks; we'll pick you up there. Hurry, hurry!"

No one questioned the orders. They had all accepted his authority, tacitly placed the responsibility for their salvation in his hands. But Honeycutt didn't let himself think about the burden of that. He turned for the Baldwin, while the rest of his friends and neighbors rushed away to the south.

He yelled to Purdom, "Ben, man the spigot." And to Ashmead, "Joe, you climb up and get the boiler tank open." And to Kimbrough and Murdock, "Ollie, you and Webb work the siding switches."

The five of them moved as one, Honeycutt swinging up inside the cab. Plenty of cordwood in the tender, enough to get them the fifteen miles to Springwood; he'd stacked in a fresh supply a few days ago, in anticipation of his downtrack test run. He leaned down to open one of the tank boxes, pulled out an oilcan. Which of the others for fireman? he was thinking. Ben Purdom was likely the best choice; he'd been head of the rail crew at the mill for the past couple of years. But Ben had weak lungs—

A voice said from below, as if its speaker had been privy to his thoughts, "You're gonna need a fireman, Sam. And I'm your man."

Honeycutt straightened, looked out and down.

The voice belonged to Will Denbow.

2

Dembow caught the handbar on the side of the cab, got his left foot anchored on the running board, and launched himself up through the gangway to the deck inside. He limped past Honeycutt to the tender, half turned then to face the old man.

"There's no time to argue, Sam," he said grimly. "I can handle the job, don't worry. I'm *gonna* handle it."

Honeycutt's seamed face was expressionless. His eyes bored into Denbow's for three or four seconds; then he nodded once, said, "All right, son, load her up," and turned immediately and climbed down from the cab to oil up.

Denbow was relieved and a little surprised. He'd expected an argument. The need to take the fireman's job had come over him when he'd stumped up outside—Rose on one side of him and Pete Weidenbeck on the other, helping him run— and Honeycutt began shouting out his orders. The lives of ninety people were at stake, people who'd once been his friends—that was part of it. But there was more to it than that. He wanted the fireman's job, *had* to have it, because it was something he could do even with one leg; it meant being useful again. His home was about to be wiped out; what else did he have left except the chance to be a whole man again for a few hours?

He took an armful of cordwood from the tender, pivoted on his good leg, and drove his wooden one against the pedal on the floor in front of the firebox. The butterfly doors slapped open. He dumped the cordwood in, turned back to the tender to repeat the process. The peg leg wasn't any problem now, but he'd have to be careful to watch his balance once they were in motion. He was not going to let the stump keep him from seeing this through.

Through the side glass and the narrow, oblong front glass panels, he could see Murdock and Kimbrough manning the siding switches. He could also see that the entire eastern slope beyond the yard was ablaze. Columns of smoke danced above the heaving span of flames, altering direction high up in the thin gusts and drafts of wind. The smoky heat burned in his lungs; he tightened his jaws to keep himself from coughing.

Fleetingly he thought of Rose, wondered if she was all right. She'd tried to stop him when he started for the locomotive, but he had pushed her away, yelled at her to go with the others. That damned Kincaid had taken her arm and pulled her along. She would never stop thinking of him as a helpless cripple, would never stop believing he had to be watched over and protected. Well, for a little while *he* was going to be the one to do the protecting.

Water began gushing into the boiler tank; he could hear the hissing metallic sound it made. He had the firebox half full now. He was dumping in another armload of wood when Honeycutt came up beside him again. The old man fired up the boiler, lit the lamp that hung from the paneling on the front bulkhead, and began turning valve handles and opening cylinder cocks and checking the manifold gauges. When the water gauge told him the tank was full, he leaned out of the side window to shout at Purdom and Ashmead, "Okay, shut her down!"

Denbow watched the steam gauge, high on the boiler butt. The needle climbed slowly. The glow inside the firebox flared a hotter and brighter red each time he pedaled open the butterfly doors, and the cab filled with an increasing volume of noise—the blast of the firebox, the stuttering clamor of the valves, the staccato beat of the exhaust.

He called across to Honeycutt, "About ready, Sam?"

"Pretty soon. Keep loadin'."

Another half minute went by. Then Honeycutt took his eyes off the steam gauge, called, "Ready!" to Denbow, put the headlight on, released the brakes, and wrapped his left hand around the throttle. Gave her some steam to get them moving. The drivers clanked and commenced to turn; the

Baldwin jolted forward, hissing steam, its wheel flanges sliding noisily on the rails.

They rolled over to the main track, through the open switch, and uptrack a ways past the switch for the east siding. Now Denbow could see the rest of the townspeople strung out on the west side of the right-of-way, their bodies outlined in the hellish glow of the fire. He dragged his free arm across his sweating face, swung around to the tender for more wood.

Murdock came running up alongside the cab as Honeycutt slammed the throttle shut and notched open the reverse lever between his knees. The big Baldwin shuddered, came to a stop for an instant with smoke feathering back from its stack, then began to grind backward.

"Sam!" Murdock shouted. "What about those two boxcars? They're blocking the coaches. Haul 'em out of the way, or couple 'em on and then pick up the coaches?"

"No time to waste," Honeycutt yelled down to him. "We'll have to take the boxcars with us. Couple 'em on!"

CHAPTER 8

1

FROM THE SOUTH SIDE OF THE YARD, WHERE HE WAS CLUS-tered with the others, Kincaid watched through watering eyes as the locomotive reversed its course and headed onto the siding to the two sealed boxcars. Smoke belched from its stack, blending with the sooty pall that undulated across the sky. It seemed to be moving without sound, rendered mute at this distance by the hum and roar of the conflagration.

The fire was awesome now. The slopes and ridges to the west, north, and east were solid masses of flame; red-tipped tongues licked toward the backs of the houses and cabins on the hillside beyond Main Street; patches of dry grass on the valley floor had already been blackened and some of the shade oaks had blazing crowns. Holocaust—one almost biblical in its destructive force. It made him feel as though the entire world were being incinerated.

In his mind was an image of what would soon happen to his little valley over east—his cabin, his cattle, his horses, everything he owned and everything he had built. Destroyed in one rushing sweep of flame, as if none of it had ever existed. He felt a bitter sense of loss. And yet, if he survived this night, there was nothing to stop him from rebuilding it all somewhere else, on a different piece of ground. He had started with nothing before; he could do it again. Easily, if he had a woman like Rose Denbow to build it for. . . .

The wind and heat beat against his face. The smoke not

only stung his eyes but swelled his throat and made breathing painful, as if he were trying to draw a fiery semisolid matter into his lungs. All around him men and women and children were coughing, gagging, retching.

One of those bent double not far away, he realized suddenly, was Rose.

He went to her, took her shoulders gently, and held her until she was able to stop the paroxysms and straighten up. When she looked at him, he saw that her eyes were dulled with pain and fear, her face streaked with dried sweat, dried tears. A tenderness welled up inside him, so sharp that it was like a physical ache.

"Rose," he said.

She stepped back out of his grasp. "Please, Matt—don't."

Mutely he watched her turn to stare uptrack at the locomotive. He sensed she wasn't so much watching the work there as looking for her husband. Fretting about Denbow because, after all, she still loved him?

If I had a woman like her to build it for . . .

Kincaid's hands clenched. Impotently he stared uptrack himself, past Rose's rigid body. Silhouetted against the smoky firelight, the locomotive was coupling onto the forward of the two boxcars. He could see one man working there, another man back where the coaches were, Sam Honeycutt leaning out of the cab. Honeycutt. Couldn't be a better man in charge. He had spent his entire life on and around trains, and he had already proved that he was capable of an iron will and a clear head. If anyone could get them out of Big Tree alive, Honeycutt was that man.

But Kincaid couldn't just keep on standing here, wanting to do something, feeling helpless because there was nothing for him to do. He turned, hacking, trying not to gag, and moved away along the tracks to the south.

Some of the people were kneeling or sitting on the dusty ground; others were jackknifed forward, racked by spasms of lungs and bellies. Melissa Weidenbeck convulsed beside her husband and vomited at his feet. One of Ollie Kimbrough's young daughters screamed hysterically in his arms. The edge of panic, dulled by the hope Honeycutt had given them, was sharpening again as the seconds ticked away and the smoke and heat intensified and the fire closed in around them.

Kincaid saw the two rough-clad strangers standing apart from everyone else, remembered that the heavyset one, Patch, had a crippling horror of fire. Patch still seemed to be transfixed, his eyes wide and staring at the inferno on the east slope. His mouth hung open and a glistening trail of saliva ran from one corner of it down over his chin, onto the front of his shirt. He was coughing steadily, with sounds that were like the barks of a feeble dog. The other man stood with his knuckles against his thighs, and on his face was an expression of anger and the same sort of helplessness Kincaid was feeling.

The lean man grew aware of Kincaid's gaze on him, met it for a few seconds, then deliberately shifted his body around and walked over closer to the right-of-way. Kincaid frowned, started after him, changed his mind when he remembered something else: He hadn't seen Austin Trace anywhere among the townspeople, hadn't seen him at all tonight.

Frank Bixby, the night watchman on the mill gate, was down on one knee nearby. Kincaid went to him, helped him up. "Frank," he said, "what happened to Trace?"

Bixby looked at him in a half-stunned way, said between coughs, "The old man? Christ, I don't know. Isn't he here?"

"No."

"Maybe the explosion got him."

"Maybe so," Kincaid said. "Tell me this: Why was that big freight wagon coming in so late?"

"Delivery of personal goods. Driver had a note from Trace."

"A delivery an hour past midnight?"

"It's happened before."

"What kind of personal goods?"

"I didn't ask. None of my business."

"How many men on the wagon when it drew up?"

"Just the driver."

"Heavyset, bearded man?"

"That's right."

"You didn't see anybody else?"

"No."

"How about inside, over by the powder shed?"

"I was opening the gate for the wagon," Bixby said. "Everything was quiet, then the shed just blew. What—"

A sudden shout went up from the people uptrack. Somebody yelled hoarsely, "They're coming!"

Kincaid swung around, and the things Bixby had told him were crowded into the back of his mind. Uptrack, the locomotive, its headlight glaring through the roiling smoke, was on its way out of the east siding with the two boxcars and the two coaches coupled on behind.

2

When the old Baldwin cleared the open siding switch onto the main spur, Honeycutt opened the throttle another notch with his left hand and then dropped the hand to the knob of the air-brake lever inside its slotted disk. He put his head out the side window, looked back along the string. Kimbrough and Murdock were hanging out on that side, one standing on the coupler knuckles between the second boxcar and the first coach, the other on the plates between the coaches. They both swung their free arms high over their heads to let him know everything was all right back there.

Honeycutt brought his head back inside, craned his neck to look past the throttle bar at Will Denbow. With the firebox full for the moment, Denbow was sitting on the cab seat, resting, his body bent forward tensely. His face, backlit by the glow of the fire, looked grim and capable.

Honeycutt nodded to himself. He had had to make a snap judgment about Denbow earlier: Could he handle the job? What he'd seen when he stared into the young man's eyes convinced him that he could. He was even more convinced of it now.

He smothered a cough, ducked his face against his shirt-front, and squinted through the front panel. Ahead, most of the townsfolk were packed together in a long, ragged queue, moving, gesturing urgently; a few of them had splintered off

and were staggering uptrack toward the oncoming Baldwin.
The fire had surged beyond them to the west, was racing
toward the southern end of the valley. Back north, some of
the buildings and the few abandoned wagons along Main
Street were burning. Honeycutt forced himself not to think
about his own house, everything he and Martha had in the
world except their lives. Concentrated instead on the lay of
things downtrack.

In another few minutes the way through the pass between
the southern slopes would be blocked by converging walls of
flame. And inside a half hour there wouldn't be much left of
Big Tree except charred and fiery rubble. But getting clear
of the valley didn't end the threat to them, not by a long shot.
They still had to run a twelve-mile gantlet of dense timberland, still had to cross a couple of short bridges over creek
beds and washes and the spidery trestle that spanned the
Miwok River. The more momentum the fire gained, the faster it would spread. When it got hot enough, it would hurl
whole trees, like gigantic torches, a mile or more ahead of
it, build enough speed so that even a train would be hard-
pressed to outrun it.

The Baldwin was something else to worry about. She ran
along fine at low speeds, with gentle handling; but he was
going to have to push her most of the way, keep the steam
up to its full working pressure of two hundred pounds as long
as the water lasted. The repairs he had made were intended
only to get her running again, so she could be worked on
proper at the roundhouse in Springwood. Aged and little-
used rods and valves might blow, the boiler might blow, a
dozen other things could strand or wreck them . . .

Honeycutt shook himself. No damned use in dwelling on
what could go wrong. Take things as they came, one minute
at a time.

The Baldwin's blunt nose was coming in on the first of the
running people. The headlamp bathed them and the clustered
line of the others beyond in a smoky white glare. Honeycutt
closed the throttle, jerked the whistle pull to signal Kimbrough and Murdock, who were manning the hand brakes
on the cars, and then worked the air-brake lever. He saw the

rest of the townsfolk surge toward him in a body, some of them with their mouths agape, making sounds that he couldn't hear for the hoarse intake of the air pump, the low shriek of the brake shoes binding against wheel rims, the constant barking of the exhaust. Then the Baldwin was past them all, and he brought it to a hard, jolting stop.

He set the brakes, swung off his seat. "Stay put and watch the firebox," he called to Denbow. Then he caught the side bulkhead, levered himself out through the gangway, and dropped down amid thin jets of steam.

A wave of heat and acrid smoke buffeted him; his lungs constricted and he was racked with a fit of coughing. He dragged his handkerchief out, held it up to his mouth, then started uptrack to where his friends and neighbors were massed at the darkened cars. He stopped abruptly, relieved, when he saw that they weren't fighting each other, that they were letting the women and kids in first. Matt Kincaid seemed to have taken charge, and Ashmead and Purdom and Cletus Boone were helping him hand people up the portable side steps on each of the coaches. Steam and smoke swirled around them, half obscured the tracks and the yard.

Honeycutt retreated, climbed onto the running board again, and hung there looking back. All the women and kids were aboard now; the men were starting to clamber in after them.

When there were fewer than twenty men left outside, Honeycutt pushed back up onto the cab deck. Denbow was stoking again; the butterfly doors on the firebox were open and his bent-backed frame was limned in the bright, ruddy glow from within. Honeycutt slid his buttocks onto the seat, peered through the glass to the south. The fire fronts were converging rapidly on the low granite walls of the pass—too damn fast.

We've still got time, he thought. We'll make it.

But it's goin' to be close.

He laid his hand on the air-brake lever, muscles knotted and aching with tension, and took a look back to the rear. The last few of the men were just disappearing inside the cars. Seconds later he saw Kincaid lean out of the forward coach, Cletus Boone out of the rear one. Both men signaled with frantic waves of their arms.

Honeycutt pulled the whistle, released the brakes, and opened the throttle.

The Baldwin jerked, began to roll again. Couplers banged and rods clanked and smoke poured from the stack. Watching the steam gauge, he opened her out one notch, two, three—felt her begin to hum and pound around him, creating a thunderous pulse that drowned out the thrumming of the fire. His blood began to pump faster, as it had in the old days when he was at the throttle and commencing a highball run. He gritted his teeth, put his head out again to stare downtrack.

The end of the yards loomed ahead. Beyond, to the west, where the last of the houses and cabins were located, the fire had churned to within sixty yards of the right-of-way. And on the east side, the rolling meadowland that stretched away to the pass was sheeted with flame all the way down to within twenty yards of the tracks. The pass's fractured rock walls dead ahead shone a pulsing, reflected red, like superheated metal in a forge.

Honeycutt opened the throttle another notch, watched the flames and the glowing walls hurtle toward them.

3

Rudabaugh was thrown back hard against the cracked leather seat when the train jerked into motion, then thrown hard forward and to the right as the coach shuddered and swayed. His shoulder jarred into Patch, sitting next to him at the window, and Patch made a grunting noise but didn't look his way. Didn't even turn his head from the window glass and the fire raging outside.

The train picked up speed. Rudabaugh grabbed on to the seat in front of him, steadied himself as the coach commenced to vibrate. Glass panes rattled, the floorboards and walls creaked and chatttered. Firelight flickered through the cars, created twisting shadow patterns that gave the people around him an unreal look. Kids wailing, women sobbing, everybody else choking and gasping . . . it was all like a crazy nightmare.

There were burns on his arms and legs, on his face, on his scalp—none serious, but all of them together making his body ache and sting. But at least the smoke and heat weren't so bad in here. Not yet, anyway. He could almost breathe again without pain and he didn't feel as if he were going to puke at any second, the way he had outside.

He tried to pull his thoughts together. He'd never been afraid of much except a hangrope, and he wasn't afraid now. Yet that fire out there, the way it moved and ran wild . . . he'd never seen anything like it and he couldn't seem to come to grips with it. He felt confused, powerless, as if he didn't have a handle on his own life anymore—the same way he'd felt those two years in Deer Lodge, his only time in prison.

Then there was Patch. Bastard's fear of fire was so strong, he was out of his head; couldn't think or talk, didn't even know where he was, seemed like. If he stayed that way until they got clear, it wouldn't make any difference. But if he panicked again the way he had earlier, he might do or say something that would give them away. Rudabaugh had tried to talk to him while they were waiting beside the tracks, make him understand the need for caution. But Patch had just stood there, staring at the fire. Hadn't even moved when the spasms came and he puked on himself.

Rudabaugh would have shot him then and there, if he'd had the chance; his Colt was still pouched at his hip. But there hadn't been a chance and it didn't look as though there was going to be one anytime soon. All he could do, for the time being, was to wet-nurse Patch along, watch him every second and make sure none of these people got close to him. Particularly that big redhead up in the front part of the car, the one who'd helped him get clear of the mill. Rudabaugh didn't like the way that one kept looking at them, as if he were getting ideas.

The train continued to gather speed and the coach kept on rocking and swaying. Then the flickery light inside got brighter, lit up the whole car, and all at once the people on the left-hand side were crying out. Rudabaugh saw nothing outside those windows except fire. Up close, not more than a few yards away.

He held tight to the seat in front of him; he could feel his scrotum shriveling. One of the kids screamed. Patch swiveled around beside him, leaned across in front of his body so that Rudabaugh smelled the hot puke-sour odor of his breath—

The forward windows darkened suddenly to a dull red glow. Then all the windows darkened, like a chain of lights going out one by one. The goblin shadows deepened, took over the car again. Outside now, Rudabaugh saw walls of jagged bare rock. He let out an explosive breath, heard the same relieved sound coming from all around him as he sagged backward against the seat. Dripping sweat blurred his eyes; he let go of the seat back and swiped them clear with his sleeve.

Patch was still leaning forward, hands splayed out on his knees. There were no more flames for him to watch, but he looked as if he were still seeing them: The one eye nearest Rudabaugh seemed as big around as the bottom of a whiskey glass. He was breathing fast, his mouth wide open, lips caked with dried drool and vomit.

Viciously Rudabaugh shoved him away. Patch blinked once, out of focus, then turned his head and pressed his face up close to the glass like a kid at a candy counter. Put one hand flat against the rattling pane and made a grunting, muttering sound low in his throat.

Rudabaugh sat rigid. An image came into his mind—the roadhouse up at Whiskey Slough—and then was gone. Gone. No roadhouse for him now, maybe not ever. No thirty thousand in gold, no ease and comfort for the rest of his days. This might be his *last* day, trapped here on a creaky coach in the middle of a wildfire. What a damn poor way for a man like him to die.

All Chavis's fault, goddamn his eyes. What had that dullard done to cause the explosion?

What had the stupid son of a bitch *done*?

4

The last Rose saw of the valley, the last she would ever see of it, was the houses and cabins burning along its southern perimeter. Somewhere in the mass of flames behind was *her* house, hers and Will's, and as the train plunged ahead between the pass walls, she felt the pain of her loss. A part of her life had ended tonight, and she could never reclaim it.

And yet she also felt a kind of spiritual release that, oddly, carried with it little grief. It was as if all her bridges were truly being burned behind her.

She turned her head from the window, looked down at her lap. Her hands moved on the soiled blue gingham of her dress; she could not seem to keep them still. Her fingers felt dry, papery, when she rubbed them together, vaguely numb in the knuckles and joints. The same numbness seemed to have gotten into her mind, too, giving her thoughts a detachment that was almost dreamlike.

The train was going very fast now, it seemed, and the car pitched, rolled, made loud vibrating sounds as though it would shake itself apart. But she mustn't worry about that. Sam Honeycutt knew what he was doing. And Will knew what he was doing, too—at least right now he did, acting as fireman up there in the cab with Sam. Joe Ashmead had told her that that was where Will was and what he was doing.

This was Will's element, she thought. He would be all right. But afterward, if they survived? Would his bitterness and indifference return, to make him a total cripple again?

Shimmering light illuminated the windows, filling the car. Rose lifted her head to look out on one side, then the other. The rock walls had slid past; they were clear of the pass now. The hillside to the east was blanketed in smoke and flame. The one to the west hadn't started to burn yet, but when she edged around to peer behind them, she saw fire flowing in vast waves down the ridge above the pass. A tremor went through her. She put her eyes back on her shaking hands, watched them flutter against each other, and listened to the fast, rhythmic pounding of the wheels.

When next she raised her head, she was aware of Matt

Kincaid watching her across the aisle. She didn't meet his gaze. She had avoided looking at him since they boarded the car. She knew what she would see in his face, his eyes, and she did not want to face it now.

She thought again of Will, up there in the locomotive.

She could almost feel Matt's gaze caressing her.

And deep inside she understood, even though she was not ready to admit it to herself, that she had already made her decision. That she knew which of them she would choose, if and when the time came.

CHAPTER 9

1

DENBOW FINISHED REFILLING THE FIREBOX, CHECKED THE steam—holding at one-eighty—and sank onto the fireman's seat to rest and mop sooty sweat from his face. His back was stiff from the twisting and bending; the stump of his right leg throbbed with pain. The air was clogged with cinders and smoke, and the heat from the box and from the firewind was intense. His skin felt blistered, his lungs as though they were being scraped with hot sandpaper.

Honeycutt had the throttle wide open, and the whir of the drivers, the beat of the trucks, the houndlike bark of the exhaust created a sound in Denbow's ears like that of echoing thunder. The engine and tender and the cars behind pitched and writhed in a constant sidewise motion. He'd managed to keep his balance so far, but he had to hang on to the seat or the bulkhead each time they nosed a curve and then swung onto the tangent again.

They were winding now across a long narrow valley south of the Big Tree pass, between high ridges furred with second-growth pine and Douglas fir. The headlamp made shiny humps of the rails ahead, illuminated brush-laden gullies and stretches of sloping grassland along the right-of-way. So far they had outdistanced the fire to the west, although he could see the bright glow flushing the sky over there. But the fire on the east was keeping pace with them, as if in a kind of mad race. Firebrands hurtled forward through the pall of smoke like flaming arrows. Sparks and fire devils fountained up ahead of them on that side—the same side where the tracks would eventually hook around and climb up between a cut in the long eastern ridge.

Denbow leaned forward, bracing himself, and called to Honeycutt on the high seat opposite, "Gaining on us to the east, Sam."

"Yeah, I see it."

"Try for more steam?"

"No. Safety valves are poppin' now."

Denbow knew he was right, slammed his fist against the front paneling in frustration. He could hear the valves popping and cracking, the laboring of the old cylinders and drivers. He watched Honeycutt shut down the steam a little to relieve some of the boiler pressure, heard the popping diminish almost instantly. He raised his head for another look through the side glass.

The forward line of fire seemed to be gaining faster now.

They were nearing the end of the valley; ahead, the tracks made a long thirty-degree curve to the east, and on the far side of the bend there was a short bridge spanning a dry wash. Denbow's body tensed as they started through the curve and Honeycutt kicked in a few pounds of air to take out the wobble, kicked the brakes on lightly, and then kicked them off again. But when they cut the segments and came onto the tangent, he saw that the bridge was all right; the sparks and firebrands hadn't reached it yet.

After they clattered across the bridge the fire was almost in front of them, sweeping toward the right-of-way less than a thousand yards above. The heat grew even more intense, dried his sweat the instant it came out of his pores; the hot smoke flooding his lungs made him feel light-headed. The tracks climbed gradually toward the ridge cut, but the cut itself and the line through it were obscured. All he could see was roiling smoke and spear tips of flame, and above that, in the far distance, the pine-dark summits of distant peaks silhouetted against the red-black sky.

A hundred yards ahead, something came running out of the twisting gray mass—something alive and on fire. A deer, a big buck. It staggered as it came near the rails, commenced to run around in pain-maddened circles, and finally toppled over, dead or dying. The flames turned it black and shapeless in the moment before the locomotive lunged past it. Denbow's stomach heaved. He could smell, or thought he could smell, the sickening half-sweet odor of burning hair and cooking flesh.

Their speed decreased as the grade steepened. Honeycutt opened the steam again and the engine and the cards bucked, jolted, regained a measure of the lost momentum. Cinders from the belching stack fell beside the cab like a thin black rain. Visibility ahead was less than a hundred yards and closing.

Denbow squinted at the steam gauge, pushed off the seat, and staggered, gasping, to the tender. Braced himself against its bulkhead and took out more cordwood. A wave of nausea struck him as he turned back to the firebox, nearly made him black out. For the first time his peg leg slipped on the cab deck, pitched him off balance; he went down hard on his left buttock.

Sticks of cordwood bounced and clattered through the cab. Denbow kicked one of them aside with his good leg, beat at his stump with both hands; the pain cleared away some of his dizziness. He reached to grab the seat and haul himself erect.

Honeycutt was looking across at him. Between hacking coughs he called, "You all right, Will?"

Denbow gestured that he was, pawed at his stinging eyes, twisted around again to the tender. Got another armload of wood and this time made it to the firebox without stumbling. He opened the butterfly doors and fed the blaze inside.

Outside the cab, the smoke flowed around them, seemed to enwrap the train. It was as if they were struggling blindly upward through a poisonous gray gelatin. Panic clawed at Denbow. They couldn't keep breathing much longer in thick smoke like this; they'd both pass out. Runaway train then, derailment on one of the downslope curves . . .

Seconds that seemed like minutes crawled away. Then the laboring pull of the engine ceased; the Baldwin rocked and the front boxcar banged against the tender as she leveled out and then surged ahead. The smoke on Denbow's side of the cab was shredding. He blinked, scraped at his eyes, blinked again—and had an impression of jagged slabs and ribs of granite rock in the smoke rifts.

The cut . . . they were into the ridge cut.

Honeycutt was bent double on the high seat, still coughing in spasms, and his face was a glowing, sooty bronze in the light from the cab lantern. But he was all right: His teeth were bared and his left hand was wrapped tight around the throttle, shutting it down a notch to even out their speed when they started on the downslope run.

Denbow clung to the bulkhead. The smoke in front of them was breaking up, too, and the brightening glare of the headlight showed him part of the tracks ahead, the wooded slopes to the west and the high rock shoulder to the east. The terrible blasts of heat had lessened. There was oxygen in the air again; the sweetness of it in his heaving lungs was like an elixir.

They pounded through the cut and headed into the descent on the far grade. Denbow pushed along the bulkhead to the gangway, leaned out to look behind them. There was no sign of flames on any of the cars in the string; none of the flying sparks and cinders had settled on them. Wildfire swept all along the northeast rim and on the ridges and hollows beyond. But to the southeast, paralleling the right-of-way, ragged granite formations and volcanic earthflows stretched out and down for at least a third of a mile. Madrone and salmonberry shrubs and a few pines grew there—too sparsely for the fire to take much hold. That section of terrain wouldn't check the onrushing flames for long, but maybe long enough for the train to clear the trestle across the Miwok River, three miles down the line.

When they nosed into the first of the downslope curves, he hobbled back to the firebox and checked the steam. Holding. The grade wasn't steep enough here for Honeycutt to have to use the brakes, but he had his hand on the lever, anyway. He had opened the side window again, to let hot streaming air, half smoky and half fresh, swirl through the cab.

The old man hawked deep in his throat, spat phlegm through the window. Then he called hoarsely, "Cars okay on your side?"

"Look to be."

"Thank God. It was close back there."

"Too close. We'll make it now."

Honeycutt grimaced. "Don't get cocky, son. We got a long way to go yet."

"The river'll slow the fire on the west," Denbow said. "We can outrun it from there . . . it's less than seven miles to Springwood."

The old man didn't respond. He sat still for a time, staring at nothing, as if he were thinking ahead, fretting. Or praying.

They came through the first curve, wound into the second. The grade began to level off. Denbow looked at the steam again, saw that it was dropping a little, and swung once more to the tender. The heat from the ballast lashed at him when he pedaled open the firebox doors; a fragment of burning wood popped out and stung his right cheek, dropped to the front of his shirt. He didn't take the time to slap at the smoldering cloth until he'd fed the blaze and was turning back to the tender.

At the bottom of the grade the tracks hooked southeast around the long section of rock, then looped back to the southwest across a series of hillocks and short, shallow vales. By the time they were halfway across, less than two miles from the river, the fire to the east had fallen well back—but the west fire was coming on fast, closing in on them. Denbow could see billows of smoke and leaping vanguards of flame beyond the right-hand gangway, as near to the tracks as five hundred yards.

He thought about the trestle, as Honeycutt must have been doing all along, and an icy desperation came into him. The trestle was built almost entirely of wood; one small firebrand could touch it off. And it would burn like kindling, within minutes become a collapsing black skeleton. The drought had reduced the river to a sluggish trickle; it flowed a hundred feet below the trestle, between sheer rock walls that were impossible to scale. If the trestle was burning when they got to it, they would have nowhere to go.

He remembered the deer that had come running out earlier, the fire on it and the stench of its cooking flesh. And shuddered. And went again to the tender even though the steam was back up and the firebox was nearly full.

The Baldwin thundered ahead, shaking from side to side as if it were trying to break loose from the rails. The safety valves were making intermittent popping noises again, but Honeycutt didn't shut down the steam this time. And Denbow didn't quit stoking; he kept the box full and the ballast at white heat.

One mile to the river now.

One mile to that spindly wooden trestle.

2

Patch couldn't see the flames any longer—and inside his head his father stopped screaming.

His father was dead and they'd put him out; the fire was out.

The images of that night long ago faded. Thoughts began to tumble together, his senses to work again all at once. Pain in his chest, the sour taste of vomit in his mouth, the sounds of coughing and crying and metal grinding on metal like a throbbing rhythm in his ears. He stared around him, realized with dull amazement that he was sitting in a shadowed, moving railroad car with dozens of people he didn't know and Clee Rudabaugh beside him. He couldn't remember anything about a train. All he remembered, and that dimly, was somebody grabbing him away from a spring wagon and then Rudabaugh slapping him. There was nothing else in his memory but the fire, fire everywhere, and his father screaming and dying while he and his mother looked on.

He tried to say something to Rudabaugh but his jaw flapped mutely. When Rudabaugh saw him doing that, his eyes narrowed and his face—burned face, hair singed off, *Jesus*— drew tight. He caught Patch's arm, held it tight.

"You know who I am?" he asked in a harsh whisper.

Patch managed a nod.

"All right, then, listen to me. We're on a train, the people in Big Tree put a train together and got us out of there."

"The explosion . . . the fire . . ."

"Shut up about that. That's all behind us. We're on our way to a place called Springwood, a safe place. You understand?"

Patch understood. But there was dim flickering light in the car, firelight, and a haze of smoke. He twisted to the window. Smoke all over the sky. And flames, he could see the flames soaring again—

Rudabaugh's other hand caught his shirt, jerked him around roughly. "Don't look out there. The fire's no danger to us now."

Patch tried again to talk, finally got words out in a voice that cracked and didn't sound like his own. "Clee . . . it's comin', I can feel it comin'."

"No. I tell you it's behind us. *Listen* to me!"

Patch's hands started to tremble. He wanted to look back at the fire, didn't want to look at it, had to look at it, wouldn't look at it . . .

"Bend forward, put your head down on your knees," Rudabaugh said. "I don't want you looking out that window no more."

"Clee . . ."

"Do it!"

Patch did it. He closed his eyes, but as soon as he did, the rocking motion of the car, the smell of smoke, made him dizzy and sick to his stomach. He popped his eyes open, gagged but didn't let anything come up.

Rudabaugh leaned down close beside him. "Stay like that. Don't raise up until I tell you to, and don't say anything to anybody—not here and not when we get to Springwood. I'll do the talking for both of us. Hear?"

"I hear," Patch said.

He sat there with his cheek resting on one knee, hands clasped on the back of his head. The noise and the motion blended together to dull and jumble his thoughts again. Fire comin' outside, he knew it was . . . but it hadn't gotten them yet . . . Springwood, a safe place . . . wasn't goin' to get him the way it had his father, wouldn't *let* it, wouldn't die the way the old man died . . .

In the back of his mind his father shrieked again, just once, and he saw the hungry flames.

3

Across the aisle, two seats behind, Kincaid watched Rose comfort a sobbing woman whose name he didn't know. The woman's husband evidently had been away from Big Tree on one of the logging crews, and she had no idea if he had been trapped by the fire or had managed to escape. When the smoke outside surrounded the car a little while ago, during the climb to the ridge cut, and all but suffocated them for long agonized seconds, the woman had become nearly hysterical. Rose had gone to her as soon as they reached the top of the grade and the smoke started to break up outside.

That was the kind of woman Rose was: caring, selfless. He could not take his eyes off her.

Watching her, thinking about her, made the waiting a little easier. So did the fact that now the fire to the east had dropped behind them and they were well out in front of the blaze on the west. Couldn't be much longer before they reached the Miwok River trestle; once they were over it, the worst part of their flight figured to be over.

But he knew that the dangers were still many. The fire might surge ahead of them if the wind picked up, reach the trestle before they did and cut them off. Honeycutt was pushing the old Baldwin at top speed, and Kincaid remembered what the old man had told him that afternoon: "She'll run. Question is, how long and how far?" And how long would the passengers be able to stand the strain *they* were under? The inpouring smoke on the grade had nearly taken more than one life. Two of the women and three of the youngsters had lost consciousness; others had been on the verge of it.

Then there were those two strangers. The one, Patch, had still been lost inside himself minutes ago when Kincaid stood up to call for windows to be opened so that crosscurrents could air out the car. But what if Patch came back to himself, panicked, and went berserk again?

Kincaid edged around to look back to where the two of them were sitting. At first he couldn't see Patch, just the lean one on the aisle; then, as the car jounced and swayed, he had a glimpse of a hunched back, hands clasped over the back of a head: Patch leaning forward, maybe being sick.

He studied the lean man for a few seconds. Staring straight ahead, with no expression on his face, but still tensed and flint-eyed in the shadowy fireglow. Hardcase type, Kincaid thought. The kind of man you wouldn't want to pick a fight with: He'd be capable of tricks to hurt you badly, maybe even to kill you.

Kincaid had known teamsters like that—but *was* the lean one a teamster? Patch seemed to be, yet an hour past midnight was a damned funny time for freighters to be delivering goods of any kind. He thought again of what Frank Bixby had told him: Patch had been the only man on the freight wagon when it drew up to the mill gate. Patch hadn't had time to drive the wagon inside before the explosion . . . but the lean man *had* been inside, had come running from the direction of the powder shed. How had he gotten into the compound? What had he been doing in there?

He was armed, too: big .45 Colt holstered on his hip. What kind of teamster carries a sidearm like that?

And what had happened to Austin Trace?

Kincaid turned the questions over and over in his mind. None of the answers he came up with made sense. The two men might be thieves, yet he couldn't imagine anything at the mill big enough and valuable enough to require an Espenshied freighter to carry away. There was also the fact that Patch had had a note from Trace. Must be Trace knew the two men, or at least who they were, and had been expecting them—

The locomotive's whistle began a sudden, urgent wail. One long blast, three short ones.

The signal for *This train is about to stop.*

Kincaid stiffened, faced front again. Felt a change in their speed that told him the throttle had been shut down and the air brakes applied. The train seemed to hurtle onward as if it were suspended in unchecked motion, like a downhill runaway. He grabbed on to the seat back in front of him. A shout went up as others realized what was happening, but the cries were lost in the savage, whining screech of brake shoes locking against wheel flanges.

The coach bucked, shuddered, plowed hard against the boxcar in front of it. A few of the passengers were pitched to the floorboards; there were more cries, the thin moaning wail of a child. The train commenced a violent deceleration, so violent that Kincaid, clinging to the seat back, was afraid a coupler would snap or a wheel would be kicked loose from a rail.

Honeycutt had applied the emergency air, was trying to bring the train to a full stop.

CHAPTER 10

1

WHEN THE BURNING TREE CAME ROLLING DOWN THE long rock-ribbed slope to the west, Honeycutt was looking straight ahead through the front glass—looking at the trestle. They had just come through a short curve, into a straight that was flanked on one side by the slope and on the other by a boulder-strewn meadow, and the trestle had appeared a third of a mile downtrack. It was stained a smoky reddish color by the firelight, but there were no flames on it anywhere that he could make out. A grim relief rose inside him.

Then he saw the tree.

The rock shoulder at the top of the slope was shrouded in smoke—a firebrand must have landed up there minutes ago, torched off the front line of pines along the crown—and the burning tree burst down out of the smoke, scattering dying tails of fire as it bounced and rolled toward the right-of-way, two hundred yards ahead of the Baldwin. It was a big, thick-trunked pine, its boughs cinder-black and wreathed in flame, part of its decaying root system still attached: a dead tree already uprooted, dislodged by the force of the blaze or by something falling against it.

Denbow saw it at the same time, yelled words that Honeycutt heard but didn't listen to. Instinctively he threw the throttle shut, reached for the emergency air. The tree bounced, hit a hooked limestone ledge that sailed it up and then down hard twenty yards from the tracks and parallel to

85

them, amid a boiling shower of dust, loose rock, and fire
devils. Momentum kept it rolling, and for a second Honeycutt thought it would roll clear of the rails before they got to
that point.

Instead it jarred *between* the lines of steel, rocked, and
settled straight along the ties as cleanly as if it had been
slotted there by design.

Honeycutt threw the emergency air wide open, bellowed,
"Brace yourself!" to Denbow, and yanked frantically on the
whistle pull.

The turbine howled, the exhaust roared, the air pumps
hammered; then the brake shoes screeched against wheel
rims and sprayed thin fans of sparks. Draft rigging buckled
as the brakes held traction. Honeycutt had his body anchored
on the seat, his feet planted on the floorboard, but the shud-
dering slide of the locomotive, the slap of the tender, and the
other cars behind, rocked him just the same; banged his head
against the side window hard enough to make him see double. Across the cab, Denbow was down on his good knee,
clinging to the bulkhead, trying to haul himself upright.

The burning tree seemed to be rushing toward them at
tremendous speed, looming massively in the white wash of
light from the headlamp. Through the open window Honeycutt saw the yellowish flames leaping up from the tree, the
bluish flames that rimmed the top of the boiler stack. There
was the taste of brass in his mouth. His heart acted as though
it were trying to burst through the wall of his chest.

Stop! he thought. *Stop, damn you,* stop!

The skidding part of the deceleration began to let up; the
wild shriek of metal on metal lessened. The Baldwin shim-
mied, seemed to want to stand on its nose. In front of them
the burning pine was fifty yards away, forty, thirty. Honeycutt couldn't see the splintered root system or the lower half
of the bole—

The locomotive's nose pilot bumped against the tree with
enough force to rock the cab to and fro like a toy.

And they ground to a quivering halt.

Pain erupted in Honeycutt's neck, gave him a fleeting fear
of paralysis before it dulled and he was able to move. Steam

hissed, valves popped like gunshots. There was the stench of hot metal, of wood smoke. He pushed off the seat, saw Denbow leaning against the bulkhead with his face pinched and bloodless beneath its coating of soot and dried sweat, but he didn't waste any time with words. He stumbled to the gangway, swung out and down, and ran to where he could see directly in front of the locomotive.

The fire-streaked pine was still jammed squarely between the rails, fifteen feet forward of the pilot.

Damn the luck!

He looked at the trestle; it was still clear of fire. Swung his gaze to the rocky incline. There wasn't anything burning on the slope itself, but across the crown, several hundred yards back, flames licked up through the thick smoke haze; and there were more flames on the barren ground that stretched down to the rim of the river gorge. Honeycutt pivoted, looked to the east. The blaze hadn't gotten to the meadow on that side, but it was sweeping fast over the hills behind it.

He dragged smoky air into his lungs, ran back to where Denbow was hanging out of the gangway. Ashmead and Purdom and Kimbrough were pounding toward the Baldwin from the rear of the train; a few of the other people had their heads poked out of the coach windows. He could hear the babble of their voices above the hissing steam and the complaining engine and the distant, humming crackle of the wildfire.

Denbow yelled down to him, "Sam—can we kick it clear?"

"No. Still sittin' smack between the rails."

Purdom shouted, "What's happened, for God's sake?" as he and the other two came running up. Honeycutt didn't answer him. His mind sorted furiously through possible options. They couldn't push the tree all the way across the trestle, even if they put out the fire on it first. Take too long: That was a damn big pine, the Baldwin was already close to overheating, and the trestle was liable to touch off before they could get across. Only one thing to do, then. Take some time to do that, too, but not as much.

He shouted to the others, "Have to move it by hand—get

the top section canted crosstrack enough so I can nose it clear.''

"By hand?'' Ashmead said. He was staring downtrack at the burning pine. "Sam, that's a hell of a big tree—''

"I don't care how big it is, there are fifty men with strong backs on this train.'' But as he said that, something else occurred to him. "The boxcars. Some kind of machine parts in 'em, might be something we can use for pry bars. Joe, you and Ollie break one of the seals, see what you can find.''

He pushed past them and ran uptrack to the coaches.

2

Rudabaugh stood in the car aisle, people swarming around him, and tried to shake the confusion out of his head. He didn't know what the hell had happened; none of them seemed to—just that they'd all of a sudden gone into a long, hard-braking skid and finally come to a jolting stop that had thrown half the passengers out of their seats.

Outside the west windows, somebody started yelling, "All the men out! All the men out! Women and children stay where you are, keep the windows shut!''

Everybody kept swarming around, as confused as he was. Then, up front, the big redhead shouted, "You heard him. All the men out, hurry up, hurry up.'' And that seemed to restore some kind of order.

The car began to empty of men. Rudabaugh hesitated, looked at Patch, and saw that he was still sitting in the same place, holding his head where he'd cracked it on something and a bloody gash had opened up. He seemed to be lost to himself again—enough so that he wouldn't do something crazy. All right, Rudabaugh thought. He turned to the front, followed the rest of the men out.

They were all running toward the locomotive, and when he got up there himself, he saw that there was a burning tree sitting in the center of the tracks, directly ahead of the engine. Christ, no wonder they'd had to brake so fast and hard. If they'd hit that tree with any speed, they'd all be dead now in the wreckage.

Smoke streamed overhead, coming from the top of a long rocky slope to the west. It started him coughing again. He could see fire up there sweeping toward what looked like a narrow canyon up ahead. There was a trestle across the canyon . . . and that told him all he needed to know about how things stood.

The old man, the engineer, was talking fast and loud; Rudabaugh paid attention. What the old man was saying was that they were going to move the top section of the tree so he could shove it clear with the locomotive. He told them to use their clothing to beat out the fire first. One of the men argued that they couldn't move a tree that size by hand, not as hot as it was, and the old man said that somebody was opening up a boxcar to look for tools they could use.

Rudabaugh glanced at the forward boxcar. Two men were working there, just sliding open the doors. Inside, he could see stacks of crates and long wooden boxes stenciled with the words ACME FOUNDRY—MACHINE PARTS. And something clicked in his mind, kept him standing where he was while the others rushed ahead to the burning tree, stripping off shirts as they went.

One of the men at the boxcar climbed up inside, fumbled around a couple of the crates, and then yelled down to the other one, "Ollie, get a hammer and chisel from the cab." The second man, Ollie, ran down to the locomotive, past a one-legged man with black grime all over him who was looking Rudabaugh's way. When Rudabaugh started toward the boxcar, the peg leg limped toward him and shouted, "You! Get downtrack and help the others!"

Rudabaugh halted, but he kept on looking at those crates and boxes inside the car.

Ollie came back out of the cab with a hammer and chisel, took them to the boxcar, and handed them up to the one inside. Climbed up beside him. Then the two of them started popping open a long wooden crate.

"What's the matter with you?" the peg leg shouted at Rudabaugh. "I told you to help the others!"

He didn't move.

The two men in the car got the crate open—and both of

them jerked as if there were strings attached to their necks and somebody had yanked them. Ollie reached inside, came up with something long and shiny in his hand.

"Jesus Christ—rifles! There's *rifles* in here!"

Now Rudabaugh knew for sure what that crazy son of a bitch Trace had done with the ordnance. He felt a savage, empty rage. And a cut of fear. They'd been dragging the weapons and ammunition and black powder and dynamite through fire and smoky heat all the way from Big Tree, and now they were sitting here with it and the fire was closing in around them, and all it would take was for the heat to reach the right temperature inside one of those cars to blow them all to kingdom come.

3

Denbow pulled up short, forgot all about the lean stranger, and stared disbelievingly at Ashmead and Kimbrough inside the boxcar.

"Rifles," Kimbrough shouted again. "Car's full of 'em!"

Behind Denbow, Honeycutt's voice demanded, "What's keepin' you men?" and Denbow turned as the old man hurried up. "Something we can use in there or not?"

Denbow said, "Rifles, Sam. Look."

"What in blazes!"

Honeycutt ran over to the car, Denbow hobbling at his side. The rifle in Kimbrough's hands looked to be a Winchester .44-40, brand-new, pieces of straw packing caught on its surfaces.

"Don't make sense," Kimbrough said. "What would old man Trace be doing with all these weapons?"

"To hell with that," Honeycutt said urgently. "What else is in there?"

Ashmead had climbed up on the crates, was peering into the gloom deeper inside the car. "Can't tell what's in the back. Figures to be cartridges, though. . . .

"Black powder? Dynamite?"

"No kegs that I can see."

Kimbrough said, "The other car," and started to jump down.

Honeycutt stayed him with an upraised hand. "Not yet. We got to get that tree off the track."

"Christ, Sam, if there *is* black powder or dynamite in one of these . . ."

He didn't finish the sentence, didn't have to. They all knew what would happen if there were explosives aboard. Denbow recollected the heat and smoke on the grade to the ridge cut three miles back, the nearness of the fire there. His stomach clenched. They never would have known what ripped them apart.

"What'll we do?" Ashmead asked. His voice was shaky now; sweat glistened on his moon face. "We can't unload the cars—there's not enough time. And we can't uncouple 'em, either, not without stranding the coaches."

Honeycutt said grimly, "Only choice we got is to clear the track and keep on goin'."

"What about the others?" Denbow asked. "Tell them?"

"We got to. They're havin' trouble movin' the tree—they need leverage."

Kimbrough said, "These rifles'll do, by God."

"That's what I'm thinkin'. Get a couple of those crates emptied. Then you and Joe check through this car, open up the other one. If you find any explosives, get 'em out if you can and dump 'em."

"Right."

"I'll handle the others." Honeycutt took a couple of steps, checked himself when he saw the lean stranger nearby. "Come on, mister," he snapped at the man, "what're you standin' around for? Get down there and help with that tree."

The stranger hesitated, then said, "Yeah, okay." He ran downtrack with Honeycutt.

Denbow looked uptrack behind the train. Clouds of smoke eddied around the curve several hundred yards distant: the fires on both sides of the right-of-way had joined somewhere back there. There was no immediate threat from the east yet, but to the west the onrushing wall was drawing dangerously close. The ridge above the rocky slope was covered with running fire.

And he thought the wind might be picking up.

He felt raw-rubbed inside; his head ached and his throat was so dry he couldn't swallow. Not much time, he thought. Fifteen or twenty minutes at the outside. Firebrand could torch that trestle any second . . .

He stared down at what was happening around the lodged tree. The other men had beaten the fire out—the pine was smoldering now, a charred black hulk—and they were struggling, without much success so far, to move the upper end of it. Some were kicking or tugging with shirt-wrapped hands at the boughs, trying to strip them off to lighten the tree's weight. Honeycutt had moved in among them, and as Denbow watched, most of the men quit working at the news of what was in the opened boxcar. He could hear their voices raised in sudden alarm. But Honeycutt held them there by force of his iron will, got all but four of them back to work within seconds. Those four he brought on the run to the open car.

Denbow joined them, saw in their faces what must be reflected in his own. None of them said anything; there was nothing to say. Kimbrough and Ashmead had emptied two of the crates, laid the rifles in the doorway, and were now climbing through the car hunting explosives. Denbow and Honeycutt loaded half a dozen Winchesters into the arms of each of the other four men for transport downtrack; and the carriers came back for more until there were no rifles left.

Kimbrough and Ashmead jumped down. "No powder in there," Kimbrough said. "Can't tell about dynamite without opening every goddamn box." He went to the second boxcar, helped Ashmead break the seal.

Denbow stumped over close by. He knew what they were going to find inside, so there was no surprise when Ashmead confirmed it less than a minute after the two of them clambered up. There were at least a dozen kegs in there, each of them marked NAILS and the one Ashmead pried open full of black powder. And they were all wedged at the back of the car, behind a pair of large crates and one massive box the size of a small wagon, so that there was no way to get them out without unloading the whole car.

In frustration, Ashmead used his hammer to rip up the boards on one of the big crates. Then he stepped back with a look of astonished fury on his sweating face. "God Almighty," he said. "A Gatling gun."

Kimbrough looked for himself. "What in hell's in that big box? A howitzer?"

Denbow listened in disbelief. There seemed to be enough firepower here to start a small war. Austin Trace was a strange, secretive man and nobody liked him much, but something like this? Rifles, explosives, Gatling guns, howitzers . . . it plain unsettled a man's mind.

And where *was* Trace, anyhow? Denbow couldn't recall seeing him in Big Tree tonight, didn't think he was on the train. Explosion or the fire must have gotten him—

Honeycutt was there again. He listened without expression to what Kimbrough and Ashmead had to tell him, then said between his teeth, "Get those cars closed up; won't be long until we're ready. And keep your mouths shut when you go back inside the coaches. I don't want the women and kids to know about this."

He prodded Denbow back toward the cab. "Will, you go up and load the firebox. I'm goin' to oil up again."

"On my way."

As Honeycutt hurried ahead to the Baldwin, Denbow noticed the other stranger, the heavyset, bearded one, come stumbling out of the first coach. But he didn't pay much attention. The smoke was thickening along the rails behind the train, thickening everywhere; it started him coughing again. The firewind blew hot against his cheeks, made them feel feverish.

He limped to the cab. Ahead, the rest of the men were lined up along the tree, working frantically with the Winchester rifles, digging muzzles and stocks down into the dirt between the ties. They'd managed to lever part of the bole up onto one of the rails. In the glare of the headlight their naked backs gleamed with sweat as they strained against the deadweight. Another five minutes, maybe, before they were able to move it far enough for the Baldwin to shove it clear.

Five minutes. And another five for everybody to get back into the coaches and the train to start moving again . . .

Denbow climbed up through the gangway. The stump of his right leg was paining him again—sharp, biting pulses. He took chunks from what was left of the stacks of cordwood in the tender, brought them over to the firebox. He could hear the men grunting around the pine, one of them shouting, "Heave! Heave!"

He pedaled open the butterfly doors, flung the armload of wood inside. The ballast was mostly ash now, but it still glowed bright red and gave off searing heat against his face. Inside the box, all around them . . . like glimpses of hell.

More wood, more wood. And all the while he tried not to think about the approaching wildfire and the heat building around what was in those boxcars.

CHAPTER 11

1

PATCH STOOD AGAINST THE SECOND BOXCAR LIKE A MAN crucified—back flattened to the wood siding, arms straight out from his body—and watched the fire coming for him.

His father was screaming again, dying again, and he wanted to scream himself but he had no voice. The terror kept him standing there now, as it had brought him lunging from the coach a minute ago. He'd come to awareness again with his head hurting and blood all over his face and hands, and Rudabaugh was gone, all the men were gone, and the train had stopped moving . . . they had stopped *moving* . . . and the flames were still close, still reaching for him. He'd lurched to his feet and out of the car. Then the heat and smoke had driven him back against the boxcar.

Why weren't they moving? He had to make them move, get away from here before it was too late.

His legs carried him sideways along the car to where it was hooked onto the second boxcar. He backed in against the coupler between the cars, crawled up over it, and swung himself around to the opposite side. But the fire was over there, too; it was everywhere; it was trying to surround him. He looked desperately to the front of the train, saw that somebody was down on one knee beside the locomotive, that men farther on were doing something with what looked like a charred tree.

He ran that way. The kneeling man heard him coming,

stood up as he neared, and called something to him. But Patch couldn't hear it for the noise of the fire and the screaming of his father. He stumbled past the man by a couple of steps, stopped and stared at the others working around the tree. Moving it off the tracks . . . it was blocking the tracks. That was why the train had stopped. Then he realized dully what it was they were using to move the tree. Rifles. Winchester rifles. But that didn't seem right, why would they all be—

A hand caught his shoulder, spun him, and he was looking at the man who'd been kneeling. An old man with a soot-blackened face that looked charred like the tree, like his father that night in the barnyard. Burned-up dead face shining in the awful smoky light of the fire.

Help me, help me!

Patch shook his head until the screaming faded. The old man was saying, ". . . the hell have you been, mister? Why aren't you down there helpin'?" But Patch didn't listen to that; he was trying to make words of his own come out.

"Tell them . . . hurry up!" he managed finally. "Fire's comin' . . . we got to get out of here!"

The old man scowled. "Pull yourself together, man."

Patch said, "Goddamn you, make them hurry!" and clutched at the old man's shirt. But the old man was strong and shoved him away angrily, with enough force to stagger him. Patch caught himself and started for him. Halted when the old man raised a big oilcan he was holding in one hand, waved it like a club.

"Get back to the coach, you damn coward. And stay there. You're not doin' anybody any good out here."

Patch wanted to take the oilcan away from him, beat him down with it. But a glimmer of reason kept him from doing it. The old man might be the engineer . . . and he couldn't fight all of them, couldn't *make* them hurry, with nothing but an oilcan and his bare hands.

He backed away, in closer to the tender behind the locomotive. The old man glared at him, then climbed up inside the cab. Patch stood there looking at the flames. Heat blasted against his face; curling smoke made him gag. And the fire moved closer, closer, reaching out for him, making his father scream louder and louder.

One of the men came running away from the tree, stopped outside the gangway. "Can't move it much farther, Sam," he shouted up. "Heat's getting bad. Those explosives could blow anytime."

"All right," the old man's voice answered. "Brace it so it's firm on the rail, signal when you're ready."

"Right."

Panic ripped at Patch, started him moving again. He backed off until he reached the end of the first boxcar.

Rifles. All of them using Winchester rifles.

Those explosives could blow anytime.

Winchesters, brand-new Winchesters.

Boxcars.

Trace, the mill, Rudabaugh saying to him at some point that the ordnance hadn't been inside the compound, supposed to be Winchesters and explosives among the ordnance—

No!

No!

He whirled, lunged over the coupler, hurled himself at the boxcar doors.

2

In the cab Honeycutt stood with his left hand opening and closing nervously around the throttle, listening to the air pump chug as the pressure built up again. The firewind and the pulsing heat of the box made it hell-hot in there, and the air was foul with swirling smoke. He'd tied his handkerchief over his nose and mouth, but that didn't help much; he was beginning to feel sick and weak-kneed. He knew without thinking about it that his sixty-five-year-old body couldn't take much more of this kind of abuse.

Beside him, Denbow leaned tensely against the fireman's seat and kept an eye on the steam gauge. He'd loaded the box full and the steam was up and they were ready to move as soon as Kincaid signaled that the men outside had firmed the tree.

Honeycutt glanced again at the water gauge. They were low on water now—the Baldwin was a thirsty hog—and he'd have to watch their speed and the boiler-pressure gauge; the last thing he could afford to risk was a boiler explosion.

He put his head through the side window. He could see the upper half of the pine, and not much more than a third of it had been angled crossrail. So he wouldn't be able to ease up to it, lock the pilot against it, and just push it off. It was liable to slide right back between the rails. What he'd have to do was ram it, pray the impact widened the angle of tilt, and then ram it again immediately and hope to spin it loose. Momentum would have to do the rest.

Farther downtrack, drifting smoke obscured the trestle; as far as he could tell, there were no flames on the framework yet. But the fire was licking along the rim of the river gorge to the west, racing along the meadow on the opposite side. The wind seemed to have picked up some, too. The trestle wasn't going to last much more than a few minutes.

They were almost ready. He strained his eyes for Kincaid's signal—

Denbow shouted, "Sam!" in sudden alarm, jerked away from the fireman's seat. Honeycutt saw him starting toward the rightside gangway, pivoted that way.

The heavyset stranger, the coward, was coming up through the gangway with a revolver in his hand.

Honeycutt froze. The coward set his feet wide apart in front of the tender, aiming the revolver—a brand-new Starr Army .44—at Honeycutt's brisket. *Got it from one of the boxcars,* Honeycutt thought; *found cartridges for it. He knows what we're carryin'.*

The man's face was wild, half mad with fear; his eyes looked as though they were on fire. "Tell somebody to unhook those boxcars!" he cried.

Denbow said, "For Christ's sake, we can't do that—"

"Not gonna blow me up—not me!"

Honeycutt could feel veins swelling in his face and neck.

There was fury in him, and fear, too—not of the revolver or the stranger, but for the safety of his passengers.

"We can't uncouple, you goddamn fool!" he bellowed. "The *coaches* are back there!"

"Get those cars unhooked, get me away from here!"

"We ain't strandin' a hundred people to save your miserable hide—"

"Do what I say!"

"Go to hell!" Honeycutt roared, and without thinking, he lunged forward recklessly to slap at the revolver.

The coward shot him.

The bullet struck Honeycutt high on the left side of the chest. The shock straightened him up for an instant, as if he'd run headlong into a wall. Then he reeled, bounced off the firebox shield, sat down hard on the deck. He couldn't see; there was a darkness, like shutters, drawn across his eyes. He heard the dying echoes of the shot, shouts, scrambling movement. Felt numbness all through his upper body, blood pumping hot against the fingers of an upraised hand.

Shot me, he thought. *I'm shot.*

Then he thought nothing.

3

Kincaid stepped back from the charred pine, threw the rifle he'd been using away behind him. They had the tree as firmed up on the rail as they were going to get it. And the smoke had thickened to the point where they couldn't work any longer; it had already felled one man, Ben Purdom, and put two others on their knees.

Coughing, Kincaid dragged a forearm across his bleary eyes, pulled the scorched remnants of his shirt from around his hands. The hands were burned, in places, anyway, from the hot wood. His shoulder was burned, too, where he'd laid it against the trunk before the discovery of what was in the boxcars. But he barely felt the pain; there was too much urgency in him.

He turned toward the locomotive, to signal Honeycutt that

they were ready. And through the gray haze he saw the heavyset stranger, Patch, swinging up inside the cab.

There was something in Patch's hand. Kincaid couldn't tell what for the smoke, but warning bells clanged in his brain. Without hesitation, he broke and ran for the locomotive.

Heard Patch yelling, Honeycutt yelling. Heard the gunshot just before he reached the running board.

He lunged for the handbar, grabbed it, hauled himself up in time to see Honeycutt falling to the deck, Denbow standing there with confusion and rage on his face, Patch brandishing a big Army-issue revolver.

Kincaid caught Patch's wrist with his right hand, slapped his left arm around the man's thick neck, and jerked him up against his own body. Denbow yelled something, tried to come to Kincaid's aid—and fell over Honeycutt. Bull-snorting, Patch first attempted to get the revolver up between himself and Kincaid and then, when he couldn't manage that, sought to rupture him with an upthrust knee.

Kincaid twisted, took the blow on his upper thigh. Levered the two of them around into the gangway. But it was like trying to hold on to a maddened animal; he could feel his grip slipping as Patch flailed wildly against him with arms, legs, body, all the while making that bullish snorting noise.

Then Denbow was there again, but Kincaid had his back to the cab, jammed together with Patch in the gangway, and Denbow couldn't reach around to get at Patch. He threw his weight against them, anyway. And the two of them went toppling out of the gangway.

Patch wrenched free in midair, so that they landed apart. Kincaid struck the ground on his right shoulder with enough force to half stun him. He rolled over, came up to his knees gagging on smoke, shaking his head to clear it.

Patch had lost the revolver in the fall, was crawling away toward where it lay next to one of the locomotive's big wheels. Close by there were shouts, confused, shuffling footfalls: the other men crowding up. But none of them was close enough to keep Patch from getting to the revolver.

Kincaid pushed off his knees in a flat, awkward dive; clawed at Patch's trailing leg; couldn't hold it when Patch kicked forward. By the time he folded himself back onto his knees, Patch had the gun. He came around with it, aimed it at Kincaid's head. There was nothing Kincaid could do but tense his body to meet the bullet in one final lunge—

A handgun went off, but it wasn't Patch's: two shots, fast-triggered, from behind and to the left of Kincaid. And suddenly there were a pair of red-black blotches on the front of Patch's shirt, one above the other.

The shouting and shuffling of the men stopped at once, as if they had all been frozen in place. Patch jerked back and up on his knees; the wildness went out of his face, leaving only bewilderment. He made a grunting sound, fell forward on top of the revolver, and lay unmoving.

Kincaid slid around on all fours.

The lean stranger was standing twenty feet away, apart from all the others, with smoke still dribbling from the muzzle of his Colt six-gun.

4

Rudabaugh retreated another couple of steps, to keep all the men within the range of his vision. But none of them made a move in his direction. Some were stricken with spasms of coughing, and the rest shifted their gazes nervously between him and Patch lying there on the ground.

They all *wanted* to move, though, he could see that. Not at him, not even away from his gun; to get into those coaches and away from here before it was too late.

It was the same thing Rudabaugh wanted. That was why he'd shot Patch. The poor damn addlehead must have found out about the ordnance and it had done him in for fair. He'd left Rudabaugh no choice but to take control of matters before they got completely out of hand.

He called to the peg leg up in the cab, "Where's the engineer?"

"He's shot, damn you."

"Dead?"

"No, but he's hurt bad."

"You know how to drive this train?"

"I know how to drive it. But I got to have a fireman; I can't do all the work myself."

Rudabaugh started to tell him to pick somebody, changed his mind when he saw the way the redhead down on the ground was watching him. Trouble, that one. Proddy. Better if he were in the cab where Rudabaugh could keep an eye on him. For the cab was where Rudabaugh intended to ride from now on.

He said to the redhead, "You—can you do the fireman's job?"

The peg leg shouted, "Not him! I want Ben Purdom!"

"Ben's too groggy," somebody said. "Smoke got to him."

"All right, then Joe Ashmead—"

"Shut up!" Rudabaugh shifted his gaze back to the redhead. "Well?"

"I can do it," the redhead said flatly.

"Do it, then. Couple of you other men tend to the engineer. Everybody else into the coaches—quick!"

He'd let them go with no time to spare. Another few seconds with that fire closing in around them and they'd have tried to jump him. Now they did what he'd told them. Three men pushed up into the cab and the rest broke for the cars. A few seconds later the three came down with the wounded engineer, carried him uptrack after the others. Then the redhead climbed up to join the peg leg.

Rudabaugh stayed where he was, fighting dizziness from the smoke, looking from the locomotive back to the coaches. Patch had begun to twitch some—still alive. But he wasn't trying to get up or use his weapon, so Rudabaugh didn't bother to finish him.

When the wounded engineer had been handed inside, Rudabaugh jumped up onto the cab's running board and pulled himself inside. He stood with his back braced against the tender wall.

"They're loaded in," he told the peg leg. "Get this train moving."

CHAPTER 12

1

DENBOW SAT ON THE HIGH SEAT, CHECKING THE GAUGES. There was no time to think about the shootings or having the lean stranger and Kincaid here in the cab with him. Or that it had been years since he'd driven the 0-6-0 switcher in the Oakland yards, and then only under his father's supervision. He'd do the job because it was all up to him now; they were all dependent on him. He felt a grim, muted excitement. It was fitting in a way—compensation for the leg he'd lost, a chance to be more than a man again.

A chance to be a savior.

The Baldwin was low on water, he saw, and the oil pressure was down and the boiler pressure was up. Worry about those things later. The steam was still up, that was what was important now. The tree—how would Honeycutt have dealt with it? Eased up to it, nosed it off? No, too much danger of it falling back betwixt the rails. Honeycutt would have rammed it, and that was what he would do, too. Ram it hard, ram it again if he had to, keep right on going with the throttle notched open.

Denbow was ready when the gun-hawking stranger told him to get moving. He didn't waste any time. He gave the whistle three yanks, signaling for Murdock and whoever was helping him now to release the rear brakes, then worked the air lever. The air pump hammered as it fought to release the clamped brake shoes. The second the hammering stopped, he sucked in a breath and gave her steam.

Exhaust churning, wheel flanges grinding on the rails, the Baldwin jerked forward. The pilot slammed hard against the bottom of the pine. That impact rocked them in a reverse motion that snapped Denbow's head back, almost knocked Kincaid and the stranger off their feet. Then there was the lunging impact of the tender and the cars behind, and his head snapped forward again as the locomotive bucked the opposite way.

Outside, the tree skidded, teetered, started to slide back.

He threw the throttle open another notch, felt the power surge, and the pilot rammed the pine again. This time, as it slid ahead, the blackened upper bole swung out at a forty-five-degree angle. They hit it a third time almost immediately, with less force; the pilot tapped it, locked against it, and the impetus of the straining engine shoved it all the way around and hurled it off the rails.

The Baldwin trembled with the release of the tree's resisting weight, and soared ahead. The forward boxcar slapped the tender again, making a booming metallic clatter. Then the string straightened out and their speed increased rapidly Smoke shredded ahead of them, fanned out on both sides. The long white beam of the headlight probed through it, finally picked out the near half of the trestle.

It was burning.

A laboring breath caught in Denbow's throat. Flames licked along the framework thirty feet below the tracks in one place out near the middle, and parallel to the tracks in another place closer in. But the fire had only just taken hold, hadn't started to race yet. *Still time to get across. And don't even think about flames leaping up around those boxcars . . .*

Denbow gave her more steam. They would hit the trestle faster than was safe, but it was a risk he had to take. The fires on the wooden framework were a much greater threat.

The headlamp brightened more and more of the trestle as they bore down on it, along with upper sections of the gorge's far wall and the dense perimeter of the timberland through which the tracks ran beyond the river. Tattered wisps and patches of red-tinged smoke drifted like tule fog inside the gorge. Then they were onto the trestle, and the weakening framework seemed to shimmy with vibrations from the tons of hurtling steel. The thunder of the wheels, the drivers, the turbine took on a hollow tone. Through the smoke, Denbow had a fleeting impression of the narrow river gleaming blackly far below, but his attention was on the nearer line of fire that threatened the tracks ahead. The flames licked erratically in the wind drafts, sending out sparks that caught on other parts of the trestle and set them to burning. Fire flanked the rails on the southernmost third of the structure, creating a gantlet for them to run before they would get clear and into the timber.

Shaking, swaying, the locomotive reached the two-thirds point and nosed between the lengthening fire lines, through flames that licked up now in the center ties. Weird smoky shadows danced crazily through the cab.

Denbow saw fire devils surge upward close to his open side glass, heard the stranger shout something and pull himself to the middle of the footplate. Denbow swiveled his head long enough to determine that the man still had his balance, was clinging to the tender bulkhead with his free hand. Then he whipped his gaze back to the front.

Fifty yards to the end of the trestle.

Heat surrounded him, so intense that his teeth ached. He could barely breathe; his mouth and throat were sand-dry. He hunched his shoulders, half expecting the explosives to let go in a blast he would neither hear nor feel.

Twenty-five yards.

Twenty . . .

And suddenly there wasn't any more fire in front of them, just the black rails and the wilderness that walled the right-of-way on both sides.

Made it!

Retching, Denbow put his head out through the side to squint back along the string. He couldn't see any fire on the boxcars on that side, or any on the coaches. When the streaming wind cleared his lungs, he pulled his head back inside and yelled to Kincaid to check the left side of the train.

But Kincaid was already at the far gangway, looking out and back. Seconds later he pivoted and called out, "No fire on this side. Yours?"

"Clear." Denbow swiped at his stinging eyes, checked the steam gauge. Pressure dropping, down to one-twenty. He felt a cut of anger and bellowed at Kincaid, "More wood! More wood, damn you, do your job if you know how!"

Kincaid gave him a quick, hard look, turned past the tight-faced gunman to lean into the tender.

The heat had lessened considerably now that they were pulling away from the trestle; the smoke in the cab was almost gone, the air almost breathable again. Sweat flowed on Denbow's body, sticking his clothes to his skin. Through the oblong front glass he saw the curve coming up ahead that would take them deep into unbroken timberland. Once they were through that three-mile-long stretch, he thought, he would open her out and hope to God the water lasted for the remaining seven miles to Springwood.

As they approached the curve, he craned outside for another look behind. Fire had claimed most of the trestle; it was already sagging in the middle, was within minutes of collapse. On this side, the tops of the trees nearest the gorge were already ablaze.

2

Down on her knees between two of the coach seats, Rose swabbed gently at the gaping wound in Sam Honeycutt's shoulder. She still didn't know what had happened to him. There had been such confusion when they brought him into the car. Martha Honeycutt had flung herself on her husband, wailing, as soon as he was laid on the seat, and it had taken two men to pull her away. Other women had cried frightened questions that were ignored; the men kept shouting for everyone to hold on, the tracks were clear and they would be moving again any second.

When they jolted into motion, she'd thought: Who is driving? Will? Is it Will? Then she thought: Where is Matt? Why isn't he here? And then she wasn't thinking at all, for they were rumbling across the trestle and there were flames shooting up around the car.

Once the flames were gone and the trestle was behind them, she had made herself stand and go to Sam, to see what could be done for him. She had had some nurse's training in San Francisco, before marrying Will; she had been called on to use it more than once since. Sam was unconscious and in shock, his shirt sodden with blood, his face pale in the semi-darkness. She'd checked his pulse, found it irregular but fairly strong. With the help of Joe Ashmead and Pete Weidenbeck, she had bared the old man's chest and gotten his head elevated and his body turned on his left side. Then she'd torn off a piece of her dress to cleanse away the blood.

God, the size of the wound! A hole . . . a *bullet* hole?

She lifted her head toward Joe Ashmead, who was squatting next to her. "Joe, for heaven's sake, he's been—"

He caught her arm, shook his head sharply. Under his breath he said, "No, don't say it. There'll be a panic."

"But what—?"

"An accident," he said in a louder voice, one that would carry. "An accident while we were moving the tree."

"Will . . . is Will all right?"

"Yes."

"He's driving the train?"

"Yes."

"And Matt Kincaid . . . what about him?"

"Fireman."

"But why would he . . . why not you or—"

"Shh. Don't fret, Rose. Can you stop the bleeding?"

It took her a moment to realize that he was asking her about Sam Honeycutt's wound. "I don't know. Without salve . . . I don't know. I'll need something to make bandages with. Nothing soiled . . . underclothing of some kind."

He nodded, pushed to his feet.

Rose closed her eyes, felt herself swaying with the motion of the train. The numbness had started to creep through her again. Then Sam moaned, and the sound brought her back to herself. She continued to cleanse his wound, watching her hands—independent creatures—moving over the old man's naked flesh. There was blood on her fingers . . . each of them sticky and stained blackly with blood.

Ashmead came back to kneel beside her, began to tear the child's petticoat he held into narrow strips.

Rose watched his hands working, her own hands working.

Sam Honeycutt shot . . . Will and Matt together in the cab . . . something wrong, something besides the fire, that she didn't understand . . . blood . . . so much blood . . .

The train hurtled onward through the long, mad night.

3

Blind with pain, Patch crawled around in the dirt beside the tracks, trying to lift himself onto his knees. Heat assaulted him in rippling waves. Smoke filled his lungs; he couldn't breathe. Inside his head there was a grayness like the smoke, swirling. And in his ears a crackling roar that grew and grew until it was a shattering pressure against his eardrums.

He didn't know how long it had been since Rudabaugh shot him; he'd slipped in and out of consciousness more than once. All he knew was terror.

The fire, coming for him—

No, please—

Coming for him!

Something hot fell on his back, burned him. He made a mewling sound that became a gasp as he twisted on the ground; his body flopped, twisted again, and he found himself on his knees. He dragged his arms up and dug fingers into his eyes, gouged them open. Grayness. And light— firelight. Flames all around him, reaching out for him.

No!

And the tracks—empty. Empty. The train was gone.

He lunged upward, reeled, fell down again. Burst of agony in his chest, blood in his mouth. A flaming cinder winked out of the grayness and struck his arm. He recoiled, beat off the cinder, vomited a thin streamer of blood, and lunged to his feet again.

No!

He stumbled forward, fell, got up, fell, got up. Black seeped in around the swirling gray at the edges of his mind. Yellow-red light bloomed massively ahead of him through the smoke, brightened; and he saw the trestle. Then the light became a line of grasping fire as high as a building, as high as a burning barn: It was all over the trestle, eating it, killing it, turning it black and shapeless and making it groan and shriek in pain.

Fire fire fire fire—

A tree limb, burning, fell out of the smoke and smote him a glancing blow across the back. And set his shirt ablaze.

He went blind again with pain, spun around and around in circles like a maddened dog chasing its tail. Couldn't reach the fire, couldn't put it out. Quit spinning and ripped at the shirt, tore it off his body and flung it away. Only by then the flames had found his Levi's, crawled up to feed on his hair and his naked back.

It had him!

He screamed.

His father screamed.

Patch and his father ran screaming out of the burning barn and up between the railroad tracks, beating at the hungry, clinging flames.

Patch and his father fell into the barnyard and lay there on the ties, writhing, shrieking, *"Help me! Help me!"*

Patch and his father, dying.

CHAPTER 13

1

In the swaying cab Kincaid stood tensely with one hip cocked against the fireman's seat, not so much resting as waiting and fretting. Wildfire, the boxcars full of weapons and explosives, Sam Honeycutt shot, Patch shot, the other stranger standing two feet away with his Colt six-gun in hand . . . all of that, and now a wild-eyed Will Denbow in control of the locomotive.

But *was* he in control? That was the question that kept worrying Kincaid's mind.

Denbow seemed to know how to drive the Baldwin well enough, and yet he was doing it with a kind of heedless abandon. He had the throttle wide open, pushing the locomotive to her limits, making her rock from side to side as if she were a steam-propelled cradle. The safety valves were popping, and the beat of the turbine was irregular, laboring, like an aged human heart that was about to give out. The manifold gauges, when Kincaid had looked at them moments ago, said that the steam was up full and yet they had less than a quarter of a tank of water left; and the boiler pressure was at four hundred pounds and climbing.

Damn it, there was no reason now for full speed and a full firebox. It was an unnecessary risk. The trestle was better than a mile behind them, Springwood was less than ten miles down the line, and the fire was no longer an immediate threat—which meant that the explosives were no longer an immediate threat, either. Except for the glare of the headlight and a faint, high flush in the sky, they were surrounded by darkness. The air was tainted with the smell of smoke, but it was clear—you could breathe it now without difficulty. There was no way the fire could catch them if they ran at two-thirds throttle; Denbow should know that better than he did. . . .

"Keep loading, Kincaid!" Denbow shouted across at him. "I want that box kept full."

"We don't need it full. And we don't need a wide-open throttle. For God's sake, man, back off on the steam, let the boiler cool down some—"

"Who the hell are you to tell me what to do?"

"Listen—"

"Not to you, rancher. You wouldn't be here if it had been up to me."

Kincaid's hands clenched. An anger that was almost hatred had welled up inside him; he could taste it like bile on the back of his tongue. He fought to control it. By nature he was not a violent man, and violence inside him was unsettling. He'd been part of enough of it tonight, seen what it could do to other men. If he gave in to it, he would lose something of himself; he would never be the same again.

He poked his head out through the left-side window. Ahead, tracks made a long gradual loop to the east, along the shore of a tiny mountain lake—one of dozens pocketed in basins all through this wilderness. The water gleamed like oil; the pines and fir trees tiered around it had an unreal appearance, like visions in a nightmare.

When he drew his head back inside, he heard Denbow shouting at him again, ordering him to load the firebox. There was nothing to be gained in arguing with him, that was plain from the look in his eyes. Reluctantly, because he wasn't sure yet what he could do about Denbow's recklessness, Kincaid moved back onto the footplate in front of the tender. He'd keep loading for now, but he'd do it at his own pace.

As he came up to the tender, the lean stranger pivoted slightly against the right-hand bulkhead to watch him. Kincaid paused, braced a shoulder against the left-side bulkhead,

He said, "Answer a question, mister."

"No questions. Just keep working."

"This is important. What happens when we reach Springwood?"

"Nothing happens unless you make it happen."

"No more gunplay?"

"I told you, that's up to you. All I'm interested in is saving my hide, same as the rest of you."

In the spill of light from the cab lamp, the stranger's face was set hard—a different kind of hardness from that in Denbow's face, like something made of stone. His eyes seemed lidless and they didn't blink much: a lizard's eyes. But unlike Denbow, he was in full command of himself. He wouldn't kill anybody else unless he was prodded into it; Kincaid believed him about that. Just what would or wouldn't happen in Springwood depended on the situation when they arrived—

"Kincaid!"

Denbow's voice again. He was swung half around on the high seat, but this time he wasn't demanding more wood for the box. He said instead, "Come over here a minute."

Kincaid frowned, glanced at the stranger, then crossed to stand next to Denbow. "What is it?"

"Something I want you to see," Denbow said loudly, and pointed to where the reverse lever was. Kincaid looked, didn't see anything out of the ordinary. Denbow bent down close beside him, and in a lowered voice that wouldn't carry above the boiler noise he said, "Time to see what you're made of, rancher."

"What?"

"We got to disarm that son of a bitch," Denbow said. There was both urgency and guile in his tone. "No telling what he might do when we get near Springwood."

"He won't do anything if we—"

"Can't take that chance. Go back over there, keep him talking. And hang on to something. I'm gonna shut down the steam and throw the air open enough to buck us and knock him off his feet. You grab his weapon, heave him out the gangway if you can do it."

Kincaid stared at him. "You want to get us both killed?"

"He won't know it's coming."

"He's not a fool and he's on his guard. It's too much of a risk."

"You gonna help me or not?"

"No. Use your head, man. We're out of fire danger now; we'll be all right if you—"

Denbow's face turned blood-dark with rage. "You goddamn coward!"

Kincaid felt the violence surge inside him, wanted to grab Denbow by the neck and shake him—and behind them the lean one yelled, "That's enough talking! Get the hell away from each other!"

The words brought Kincaid erect, made him back off a step. The stranger had come forward and was standing with his feet spread apart, left hand anchored against the cab bulkhead, right hand holding the Colt steady. His expression hadn't changed any, but his eyes were colder now, deadlier. He was not a man you could fool. No matter what the circumstances, you would never catch him unawares.

Kincaid put his gaze on Denbow again. And felt the short hairs pull along his neck. Denbow's rage was gone; his face was as expressionless as the stranger's. But in his eyes now there was stubbornness, reckless determination.

He's going to try it, anyway, Kincaid thought. *With or without my help, the damn fool is going to try for that gun.*

2

Denbow waited until they neared the long eastward loop around the lake's south shore before he got ready to make his move.

He had his left hand tight on the throttle; he slid his right over and let it rest on the air-brake lever. Then he eased around on the seat, planted his foot on the footboard, brought the wooden leg out from under the reverse bar. Kincaid, the yellow belly, was backed up against the fireman's seat, watching him with a tautness in his long body. To hell with you, Denbow thought, and shifted his attention to the hardcase with the gun. Watching him, too, that one—coldly, with his body again wedged flat against the bulkhead. The Colt six-gun was steady in his hand.

Son of a bitch had to be disarmed and thrown out of the cab, that was all there was to it. Denbow had known that as soon as he'd had time to think things through. Cold-blooded killer, capable of anything. Capable of shooting both him and Kincaid once they got near Springwood, locking the throttle open, and then jumping clear: creating a runaway that would crash and kill everybody on board, just so he could get away in the confusion. Kincaid, the damned coward, didn't want to believe in that sort of thing happening; but Denbow knew better. Making a move against the gun-hawk here and now was risky, but it was a hell of a lot less risky than doing nothing at all.

The excitement Denbow had felt since taking the throttle was sharper now. All up to him, by God. All up to a one-legged man, a cripple. He felt like laughing. Well, he'd be equal to it, just as he'd been equal to everything else tonight. He'd show them all.

He inclined his body back so he could look through the side window. Ahead, the black rails were beginning to curve beyond the reach of the headlight. In another few seconds the Baldwin would lean swaying into the curve. When he braked, the jolt would sharpen the listing angle, and perhaps that in itself would be enough to spill the stranger right out of the gangway. Knock him off his pins, anyway. Maybe make him drop the revolver.

His teeth clamped together and he set himself. The loco-motive started into the curve with a small lurching shock—

Kincaid suddenly pushed away from the fireman's seat and barked at him, "Denbow, don't do it!"

A frenzy took hold of Denbow. He thought: You dirty coward! And braced himself on the seat, threw the throttle shut, and hit the air.

There was a moment of headlong drifting motion. Then the brake shoes locked and ground and the Baldwin jarred, pulled back, shuddered forward again when the tender plowed into it from behind. Kincaid was thrown along the far side of the boiler and into the piping on the front bulkhead. The gun-hawk lost his grip on the tender bulkhead, came staggering away from it. His free hand groped out to the gangway jamb behind Denbow, his knees bent and his feet sliding wider apart as he fought to hold his balance.

Denbow was already moving by then. He came off the seat on his good left foot, twisted his body around, and slapped his left hand against the side bulkhead at the same time his peg leg came down on the deck. That held him steady long enough to swing forward again and roll his weight back onto his left foot. He came right up to the lean man, body half turned away from him at the gangway frame. Reached out for him, dug his left hand into the gun-hawk's shoulder, and threw his right against the nearest hip . . . *shove him right on through and straight to hell.* For an instant he thought he had enough leverage to do it—

Only then the stranger got his body braced and lunged back into him, brought his right elbow and forearm around in a vicious backhand sweep. Denbow saw it coming, tried to dodge, but his goddamn crutch slipped on the deck. The blow struck him full force, forearm thudding into his chin and the right side of his face, elbow cracking against his collarbone. His head snapped back; there was a flash of light and pain behind his eyes. The hardcase came all the way around in front of him, savagery in his face, and swung the Colt up and down at the same time he kicked Denbow's wooden leg out from under him.

Denbow went down. The gun barrel glanced across the side of his head as he fell, struck him again more solidly when he landed asprawl on his buttocks.

The wail of the brake shoes quit in that moment, then the bucking motion of the cab ceased. The string smoothed out, the locomotive began to pull ahead at a retarded speed through the curve and into another tangent.

Pain blurred Denbow's vision, blurred his mind, but rage and humiliation wouldn't let him give up. He dragged himself onto his left knee, tried to stand.

The stranger kicked him in the stomach.

All the air burst out of him; he toppled over backward against the footboard and lay there gasping. Dimly he saw

Kincaid standing at the controls: He'd shut off the air and opened the throttle halfway. Then the lean man bent forward in front of him, breathing hard through his mouth, pointing the revolver at Denbow's right eye.

"You try anything else," he roared, "I'll blow your goddamn head off! You understand me?"

Seconds passed before the gun-hawk straightened, backed off slowly to the tender. Denbow's smoke-weakened lungs finally dragged in enough air to let him breathe again without gasping. Some of the pain in his head and belly eased. There was oozing wetness on his right temple; he put a hand up there and then took it down and stared at a smear of blood.

"Get up," the lean man said. The savagery had gone out of his face, left it cold and hard again. "Get back on your seat."

Denbow laid a hand on the footboard, lifted himself onto it. Kincaid reached down to help him, but Denbow slapped wrathfully at the hand and said, "Get away from me, you bastard," through clamped teeth. His voice sounded as if it were coming through water. He pushed off the footboard, caught the seat, and hauled himself erect. And then threw a hard shoulder into Kincaid that sent him reeling to one side.

Kincaid caught his balance, took a step back toward him, then changed his mind and retreated to the fireman's seat. His mouth was thinned down to a slash.

All your fault, Denbow told him silently. *If we get out of this, I'll fix you. One way or another I'll fix you good.*

Denbow slid up onto the seat, wiped blood and sweat from his face, squinted at the gauges. Steam pressure was down under a hundred pounds. He notched the throttle wide open again. The Baldwin surged; smoke peppered with cinders poured out of the barking stack; the beat of the wheels and drivers once more built up to a thunderous cadence. The oil pressure was still down, too, he saw. He opened the lubricator nozzle all the way.

"More wood!" he shouted at the yellow belly. "Load up full."

Kincaid didn't move.

"More wood, I said. I want that box full."

"There's no damn need," Kincaid said. "We're less than five miles out of Springwood—"

"I'm the engineer, I know what I'm doing. You don't. Load that box!"

Behind him, the lean man said to Kincaid, "Do what he says."

"But I tell you it's dangerous—"

"You heard me. Move!"

Kincaid didn't offer any more argument. Angrily he turned back to the tender, began hauling out sticks of cordwood from the dwindling supply.

All right, Denbow thought. He put his head out to check uptrack. The fire was almost a mile behind them now; its smoky glow seemed to cover the whole of the northern sky. Downtrack, there was more dense timberland, the right-of-way walled by virgin spruce and Douglas fir. The rails ran straight for another mile, eventually came out of heavy timber near a high granite escarpment and then hooked sharply around it to the west.

All right, he thought again. The gun-hawk wouldn't be expecting him to try the same thing twice, or to try anything so soon after the first attempt, so that was when and where he'd make his next move. Right there on the curve, when the Baldwin leaned into it.

Kincaid had made him fail once, but that hadn't changed anything. He still knew what he had to do.

And this time, *nothing* would stop him from doing it.

CHAPTER 14

1

RUDABAUGH WATCHED THE REDHEAD PITCH WOOD INTO the firebox, the peg leg hunched forward at the controls. He'd thought the redhead, Kincaid, was the proddy one, the troublemaker; but the one he had to worry most about was the peg leg, Denbow. Hothead, that one. Lost a leg and thought that on account of it, he had to keep proving he was still a man. Rudabaugh had seen his type before, after the war. Yank and Reb soldiers both, left pieces of themselves on one battlefield or another—always bullyragging, looking for excuses to start a ruckus.

You could almost see Denbow's brain working, figuring some other stupid trick. Sooner or later he'd come up with something and then he'd try it. Rudabaugh didn't want to have to kill him; he wasn't sure Kincaid could operate the train. That was all that had kept him from shooting the peg leg a few minutes ago. Might come to that, though, before this crazy ride was over. He'd been damn lucky to escape the blowup at the mill, to get this far away without either the fire or the explosives finishing him. He wasn't about to let a proddy peg leg put an end to that lucky streak.

Kincaid was coming to the tender again. Rudabaugh asked him, "How far to Springwood?"

"Not far now. Four miles."

"How big a town is it?"

"How big?"

"You heard me. How many people there?"

"About six hundred. Be more now, though."

"Why?"

"Why do you think? Men gather from miles around to help fight a forest fire." Kincaid paused. "Law officers, too," he said.

"That supposed to worry me?"

"Doesn't it?"

"No," Rudabaugh said. "Get to work." Then, because Denbow was looking around at him, "You—eyes front."

Both of them did as they were told.

Rudabaugh ran his tongue over dry, ashy lips. Two choices, he thought. Ride on into Springwood, try to slip away in the confusion; there'd be plenty of horses available in town. Or drop off the train some distance outside of town. He liked the second choice much better, as long as it wouldn't strand him afoot in unpopulated and unfamiliar territory; as long as there was a ranch or farm nearby where he could steal a horse. That way nobody on this train could raise an alarm against him until after he was gone. By the time the law got around to hunting him, he'd be halfway back to San Francisco. . . .

Denbow had his head cocked around again, watching Rudabaugh with one narrowed eye. Rudabaugh didn't say anything this time, just stared back at him. After a few seconds the peg leg shifted his gaze and ordered Kincaid to hurry it up, get the goddamn firebox loaded. Kincaid ignored him. He was leaning forward in front of the boiler, studying one of the gauges.

Something between the two of them, Rudabaugh thought. They seemed to hate each other, and it wasn't just what had been going on here in the cab. But that was all to the good, as far as he was concerned: It kept them from allying themselves against him. When Denbow made his next stupid move, he'd be making it alone again.

2

Kincaid released the foot pedal to reclose the firebox doors against the white glare and blast of heat from within, then backed over to the fireman's seat and stayed there. He just wouldn't feed the ballast any longer. The safety valves were popping steadily now, like strings of firecrackers going off, and the needle on the boiler-pressure gauge hovered near six hundred pounds. She was badly overheated; the relief valves couldn't handle that kind of pressure indefinitely.

Denbow should have known that, too, but he wasn't paying any mind to the gauges or to the sounds of the valves. He was just sitting over there with his face closed tight, shouting at intervals for more wood . . . plotting.

Pretty soon the damn fool would make his second try at the lean man—it was so plain in his face that he might as well have been wearing a sign. And if Kincaid knew it, the stranger had to know it, too.

Sweat streamed from his armpits, rolled down over his naked sides. He still wasn't sure what to do. Maybe he shouldn't do anything at all. Might be best for everyone on this train if Denbow just went ahead and made another outlandish move and the stranger shot him dead. That would solve the problem of the overheating boiler.

Solve the problem of which of us gets Rose, too.

Christ! What kind of thinking was that? Fatigue and frustration and the constant tension corrupting his mind, fueling the hate he felt toward Denbow.

Outside, the sky to the east was turning a dim lavender-gray, smoothing off the heavy edges of night. Dawn was just a short time off. Twenty-four hours since he'd last slept. His body ached, his head ached. For all its negative effects, the tension, like an adhesive, was one of the things holding him together.

Suppose he went over with a stick of cordwood and clouted Denbow, took over the throttle himself? But he'd never driven a locomotive, knew too little about its operation. And suppose the lean man decided to spare Denbow because he was the acting engineer? Then it would be Kincaid who got himself shot dead.

"More wood, damn your hide!" Denbow yelled at him again.

Kincaid moved then, compulsively. Went around the boiler to stand a couple of paces away from Denbow on the high seat. "No more wood," he said. "We're almost out of water. Look at the pressure gauge—the boiler's too hot already."

"The hell it is."

"Listen to those safety valves, man. *Listen!*"

"You listen. Load up."

"I'm telling you, she's liable to blow!"

"Bullshit."

From over by the tender the stranger shouted, "What are you two arguing about?"

Kincaid said to him, "The boiler's overheated. If we don't slow, relieve some of the pressure before we run out of water, it'll explode."

The lean man scowled. "What about that?" he demanded of Denbow.

"He don't know what he's talking about. He don't know anything about a locomotive."

"I mean it," Kincaid yelled, "it'll explode!"

The stranger didn't know which of them to listen to. He asked Denbow, "You sure he's not right about that boiler?"

"Damn right I'm sure."

Kincaid said, "Come over here and take a look at the boiler gauge yourself. You'll see I'm telling the truth."

The lean man didn't move. "To hell with that. I wouldn't know what I was looking at."

"Needle's in the danger zone, you can tell that much."

"Sure she's running hot," Denbow said, "but that don't mean anything. Not yet it don't. If she runs too hot, I'll shut her down. Right now we got to have full steam; we can't afford to cut speed. Look outside . . . that fire's still close."

The stranger didn't move. But his indecision vanished, and he said, "All right, then. The quicker we get where we're going, the better." To Kincaid he said, "Get back over here. We'll keep things the way they are for now."

Desperation swelled the cords in Kincaid's neck. Damn Denbow! How could he believe what he'd been saying? Even with his feelings running wild, he ought to understand the danger—

Maybe he *did* understand it.

Maybe he was lying, playing games with a heavy-handed cunning, because a wide-open throttle was part of another reckless scheme to assault the stranger.

Kincaid turned sharply away from the boiler. Through the front window he saw that they were just emerging from the section of dense timber. Ahead was a wide granite escarpment around which the tracks curved to the west—a plum-colored mass in the early-morning gloom. Three miles exactly from there to Springwood; he remembered Sam Honeycutt pointing the landmark out to him once on a railroad map.

When he glanced down at the boiler-pressure gauge, he saw that the needle was at the six-hundred-pound line.

He backed over to the tender, trying to decide what to do. Wait it out, let Denbow make his move, hope it got him beaten or even shot? No good. Too many dangers in that, not the least of which was the boiler exploding before Denbow made his move; the popping of the valves was growing louder by the second.

"Load up!" Denbow hollered at him. "Give me steam!"

There was only one choice, Kincaid thought grimly. And he had to do it *now*, before it was too late for all of them.

He reached inside the tender for a stick of cordwood to use as a weapon.

3

Eyes narrowed, Denbow watched the escarpment loom closer beyond the Baldwin's headlight beam. In another minute they would be into the short westward curve, listing into a turn that was even sharper than the one back around the lake.

Just one more minute . . .

He leaned sideways around the throttle bar. The boiler

gauge was beyond six hundred pounds and climbing. That gutless Kincaid was right about the pressure—but not as right as he thought. A boiler like this one could stand more than seven hundred pounds without blowing. Wouldn't erupt until the pressure reached four times the working steam pressure; he knew that well enough, from talks with his father and Sam Honeycutt. There wasn't any real danger yet. Long before she got over seven hundred pounds, he'd have to shut her down and hit the air. And once he had the stranger's gun, once that hardcase was down or gone through the gangway, he'd keep the Baldwin at one-third throttle the rest of the way into Springwood.

Forty-five seconds now.

His responsibility, *his*. One-legged savior, by Christ. They'd never pity him again after tonight. Nobody would ever pity Will Denbow again.

Thirty seconds.

Twenty.

The escarpment grew, jumbled rock jutting up to block off part of the purple-black sky. Curve three hundred yards distant, flanked by the cliff and by a long grassy slope that fell away to timber, to a dry streambed thick with brush.

Fifteen seconds.

Denbow slid around on the seat, put his right hand on the air-brake lever. Worked the wooden leg into position. Boiler heat shimmered in the air, gave the interior of the cab a faintly distorted look. The locomotive groaned and shrieked as if it were in pain; the pounding rhythm of steel and steam was like a battle hymn in his ears.

Ten seconds.

And he saw Kincaid swinging around with a chunk of wood from the tender—just one chunk, held in one hand up in front of his body like a club. That, and the look on Kincaid's face, turned Denbow rigid.

Five seconds.

Kincaid took a fast, hard step toward him. A surge of fury tore Denbow's hands from the throttle and air-brake lever, drove him up off the seat. The stranger barked something behind him; he saw Kincaid jerk the stick of wood up and

ducked instinctively, left hand coming up to protect his face,
right hand launching a swing at Kincaid's head—

There was a tremendous screaming, crunching noise. And
the right side of the cab shattered like an eggshell.

Upheaval, sudden chaos. The locomotive wrenched violently, lifted, fell back; glass shattered, wood splintered,
metal tore apart; shards and shrapnel flew through the cab.
Denbow was hurled into Kincaid, and the two of them spun
in a tangle of arms and legs, struck the fireman's seat, and
burst apart. Denbow caromed into the firebox shield, striking
the lubricator on the boiler butt; it burst, sprayed him with
hot oil. He came off in a sideways stagger. Through an oil-
streaked blur he saw a huge spear of metal slash across the
cab, miss him by a foot, and hurtle out through what was
left of the front window panel.

Jesus, side rod let go—

Then something else struck him a brutal blow across the
head and knocked him senseless.

CHAPTER 15

1

RUDABAUGH THOUGHT THE BOILER HAD BLOWN UP.

The wrenching of the cab ripped him loose of the tender bulkhead, threw him to the floor with pieces of glass and wood and metal raining down all around him. Fear spiraled through him, clutched like a hand at his groin. The dynamite and black powder would blow, too—Get out of here, jump, jump!

He twisted around on the heaving deck, threw both hands up over his head. There was a gaping hole in the right side of the cab, wind gusting through it. Things had stopped flying around inside; he had a glimpse of Denbow lying sprawled out on his face with blood on his head, Kincaid up on his feet and lunging toward the controls. Then Rudabaugh was on knees and elbows, crawling through broken glass that gouged his flesh in half a dozen places, sliced open his left palm. Trying to get to the far gangway.

He didn't make it.

From down on the rails came the wailing screech of brake shoes locking, sparks flying up. The locomotive seemed to buckle for an instant, then careened wildly again and commenced to lose speed. The motion flung him away from the gangway, skidded him backward across the footplate and up against the tender. Lengths of wood flew out of it; one fetched him a glancing blow across the temple. Then there was a surging impact behind them, and the locomotive lifted again, lost more speed as it fell back, lifted a third time.

Impact, even more violent.

A tearing-metal sound somewhere.

The locomotive wrenched sideways; the left side seemed to come up off the rails. Kincaid ran away from the controls—involuntarily, legs pumping in a crazy, comic way—and Denbow's body and his own slid and tumbled in that same direction. Rudabaugh felt himself jar into the bulkhead beside the left-hand gangway, felt the locomotive and the tender spin around to the left, coming off the tracks, and then tilt and jerk farther onto that side, as if they were being flipped around and over by another toppling weight behind them.

More metal ripped apart somewhere. The locomotive kept falling and sliding sideways across the rails.

The last thing Rudabaugh heard, before he was again torn free of the bulkhead, before he went spinning into darkness, was a series of echoing crashes that went on and on and on. . . .

2

Kincaid was thrown clear.

One second he was desperately clinging to the throttle in the pitching cab, and the next he was being propelled away, and after that he was through the gangway and airborne, dropping down through clouds of hissing steam.

He landed on his feet on the slope that bordered the east side of the right-of-way, went down instantly with pain slashing through both legs, and rolled and kept on rolling over dry grass and through brush. Barreled finally into the brittle remains of a dead tree that crumbled but broke his momentum, kicked him over on his back. He slid downward another couple of yards, feet-first, before he managed to dig hands and boot heels into the turf and stop himself at the edge of a dry creek.

The sounds of rent metal filled the dawn above him. He flopped onto his stomach, stunned and dizzy, then lifted onto one knee and shook his head until his eyes focused and he could see what was happening up there.

The two passenger coaches were still on the rails, still safe—that was the first thing that registered.

They were past him by fifty yards, deeper into the curve around the escarpment, coasting to a stop, still coupled to the aft boxcar. Beyond them by another fifty yards, the forward boxcar had snapped loose from its couplers both fore and aft and had derailed; it was lying angled and broken on its side on the grassy slope. Its doors had burst open and there were crates and boxes strewn all over the slope, some still rolling, bouncing, splitting apart, and spilling out rifles, handguns, cartridges. Another thirty yards beyond the boxcar, partially hidden by the curve, the Baldwin—headlamp still burning—and its tender were just skidding to a halt, diagonally across the tracks, the locomotive upended half on its top like some huge dying animal.

Kincaid shoved painfully to his feet. He seemed not to have broken anything in the fall; he was able to run stumbling upslope. The sounds of the crash were fading now as the Baldwin and the last of the tumbling crates and boxes came to rest, and he could hear the cries of the people inside the cars. He saw Joe Ashmead and Webb Murdock swing down from one of the coaches, Murdock clutching at his right leg. None of the others had come out yet, but there was confused, shadowy movement beyond the windows.

Rose, he thought.

Three-quarters of the way upslope he turned toward the forward coach. Changed his mind, grimacing, and veered back toward the locomotive. He wouldn't accomplish anything by trying to fight his way into the car to Rose. More important, now, to find out what had happened to Denbow and the lean stranger, neither of whom appeared to be anywhere on the slope.

As he neared the broken boxcar, the incline ahead of him looked like an abandoned battlefield. Winchesters, Remington .50s, sidearms, boxes of rifle and handgun cartridges—all gleaming blackly amid splintered wood and clumps of

dry grass. No cases of dynamite, no kegs of black powder
. . . they were all inside the upright boxcar.

He ran around the derailed boxcar, up onto the right-
of-way, and then down the ties between bent and bowed
rails. Steam wafted all around the Baldwin and tender,
seemed to cling to the metal surfaces like fog, giving them
an unearthly look in the gray half-light. Torn metal made
little crackling noises. The boiler valves were still popping, but more faintly as the heat diminished; Kincaid told
himself there was little danger now of it exploding. Except
for those sounds, and the cries of the passengers behind
him, the wilderness here was wrapped in early-morning
stillness.

He looked up at the gaping hole in the right side of the
cab. He knew enough about locomotives to understand
that a side rod had let go, likely as a result of a broken
crankpin, and sliced off the feed water pumps, air pumps,
running board—everything on that side—before slashing
through the bulkhead. A miracle it hadn't decapitated one
of the three of them when it ripped into the cab.

He climbed over the undercarriage, caught hold of the
gangway frame, and hauled himself up to where he could
see inside. At first he thought the wreckage was empty; then,
when he leaned in a little farther, he spied an arm and a leg,
part of a body wedged down between the fireman's seat and
the boiler, up against the front bulkhead.

Denbow.

Kincaid pulled himself into the cab, eased down along
the canted deck until he was standing on the left-side bulkhead. He squatted there to take a close look at Denbow.
Still alive: chest moving, breath making a faint rasp
through bloody nostrils. There was blood all over his head,
a gash on the back of his skull—Kincaid had a vague memory of seeing him hit by a piece of flying woodwork, of
stepping over the fallen man to get at the throttle and the
emergency air. Denbow's wooden leg was gone, torn loose
in the crash; the right leg of his Levi's was crumpled under
the leg stump.

Kincaid probed quickly, didn't find any broken bones. Then he got a two-handed grip under Denbow's arms and tugged until he was able to prop him facedown against the deck, with his head up toward the gangway.

Outside there were voices, the sounds of people milling around. Somebody shouted, "Kincaid! You need help in there?"

"Yeah. I've got Denbow."

Scraping noises on the undercarriage, and a moment later Joe Ashmead's face appeared in the gangway. He scrambled inside the cab, dropped down beside Kincaid. Ollie Kimbrough came up to take his place in the opening.

"How bad is he?" Ashmead asked.

"Alive."

"Where's the one with the gun?"

"I don't know. He must've been thrown out after I was."

"I hope he wasn't as lucky as you."

"Yeah. Anybody hurt in the cars?"

"Few people bruised, and Jack Bennett's daughter busted her arm."

Kincaid let out a breath. Rose was all right, then. He said, "No time to waste. Let's get Denbow out of here."

He and Ashmead boosted the unconscious man up to where Kimbrough could get a grip on him. Two others helped lower him to the ground outside. Kincaid climbed out stiffly ahead of Ashmead. Uptrack he saw that everyone was out of the coaches now, running in a ragged line toward the locomotive. At the rear of the line Pete Weidenbeck and Burt Eilers were carrying Honeycutt. Near the front, her face a pale mask, was Rose.

But Kincaid stared past her, past them all—at the reddish glow in the sky to the north, paler now as the darkness grayed steadily with dawn light, but still high and smoke-crowned.

A wind had sprung up; he was aware of it for the first time, blowing sharp against his face and naked chest. And the wildfire was less than a mile away, coming fast through the timber, given impetus by the gusting wind.

CHAPTER 16

1

Running, Rose saw that Matt was one of the men standing beside the wrecked locomotive. She felt relief move through her . . . but it lasted only until she realized Will was the man lying motionless on the ground, blood streaking his face and head.

Dead, she thought. He's dead.

She ran faster, stumbling because her legs felt weak. She pushed past Matt and the other men, fell on her knees beside Will. Stared at his bloody, ravaged face. Little red frothy bubbles were coming out of both nostrils; she heard the faint, liquid inhale-exhale of his breath.

She made a sound in her throat that was half laugh, half sob. The relief stayed with her this time as she lifted Will's wrist, felt for the pulse, found it strong. There was blood in his mouth; he would suffocate if it backed up in his throat and lungs. She turned his head and pushed him gently onto his side, wiped away some of the blood with the back of her hand. Then she felt the area around the wound on his head. Skull fracture? She couldn't tell for certain.

She grew aware of movement and noise around her. People swarming confusedly. Jack Bennett's little girl wailing in pain from her broken arm. Martha Honeycutt praying aloud. Men talking in loud, urgent voices, some of them saying things she didn't understand.

"Everybody keep calm, stay together!"

"We can't get far enough away on foot. Fire'll be here before long; that dynamite and black powder will go up sure. . . ."

"Must be fire lines set up by now. They'll be out at least a mile this side of Springwood . . . digging firebreaks in those fields and meadows . . ."

"There's a logging road crosses the tracks about a mile from here, connects with one of the roads into Springwood. If we can get to that . . ."

"Stay together, stay calm."

"All right, for God's sake, let's move out."

"Everybody downtrack! Stay together, don't run, save your strength!"

Rose stood up. Most of the people, obeying orders, were hurrying away from the locomotive in a tight pack spread across the rails and ties. She saw Pete Weidenbeck and Burt Eilers lift Sam Honeycutt from where they had laid him on the ground. Saw beyond them, for the first time with recognition, the scores of crates and weapons that were scattered across the east slope. The feeling of unreality touched her mind again. Guns . . . all those guns? And something about black powder, dynamite?

Madness . . .

Someone caught her arm—Matt. Joe Ashmead and Ollie Kimbrough were lifting Will between them. She transferred her gaze to Matt. His face was battered, soot-blackened; there were burns and cuts and scrapes on his bare chest and shoulders, on both arms. Ravaged, too. But he looked . . . strong. Strong.

"You all right, Rose?"

"Yes. I . . . yes."

"Better catch up with the others. I'll help with Will."

"No, I want to stay with him."

"There's nothing you can do—"

"I've got to stay with him, Matt."

Something flickered in his eyes, seemed to deaden them for a moment. He nodded without speaking, turned immediately to help Ashmead and Kimbrough.

Supporting Will, the three men moved awkwardly downtrack in the wake of the others; Rose kept pace with them. The pack leaders disappeared around the curve in the tracks, and briefly it seemed to Rose that they were simply vanishing, walking off the edge of a precipice. She shivered. And like Lot's wife, she could not keep herself from looking back.

The pale, smoky fireglow loomed higher, closer in the dawn sky.

2

In the first few seconds after he regained consciousness, Rudabaugh didn't know where he was.

He was groggy, his mind fogged with pain. There were sharp pulses in his right shoulder when he moved. Something under him crunched and snapped, gouged at his body like poking fingers. He raised up on his left elbow, movement that brought more snapping and crunching, more pain. When he could see again, he found himself surrounded by ferns and dry underbrush, the short rocky bank of a dry creek, the mossy trunks of trees. He saw all of this clearly, for there was dusky light in the sky now; almost dawn.

He realized how quiet it was.

Not just quiet . . . a hushed, eerie stillness. No birds, no insects, no sounds anywhere except for the rustling of the wind and a faint, distant thrumming.

The underbrush was clumped up behind his head, draped over part of his body; he was half buried in it. He swept it away with his left arm, sat up, and slid around onto his knees, biting down hard against the stabbing pain in his shoulder. He was at the bottom of the slope on the east side of the tracks. He stared upslope. The train was there, on and off the rails, broken into three pieces. The boiler hadn't blown after all; something else had torn up the locomotive and caused the wreck.

The entire area was deserted, the people gone.

He smelled smoke again, and then focused on the fire raging toward him from the north. Christ—it was the *fire* that was making that thrumming noise.

Struggling, he got to his feet. His right arm hung stiffly at his side; he knew without thinking about it that the shoulder had been sprained, maybe dislocated, in his long tumbling fall down the slope. But his legs were all right. He could walk and he could run.

He scrambled up toward the right-of-way. Pain cut at him with every step, but he didn't let it slow him down. Half of the ordnance from the derailed boxcar was scattered over the slope; he looked for dynamite or kegs of black powder among them, didn't see any. That was something. With the explosives still contained inside the one boxcar, it would take longer for the fire to set them off.

But not much longer . . .

As he dodged through the scattered weapons, the thought came to him that he would need a gun. He'd lost his Colt in the wreck, and he wouldn't stand much chance of making it out of these mountains unarmed, hurt as he was. He slowed, searching for a handgun. Spied a broken crate of government-issue Starr .44s and veered over to it. He scooped up one of the revolvers, checked the action to make sure it hadn't been damaged. It took him another minute to locate a busted crate of cartridges. Clumsily—the fingers on his right hand were numb at the tips—he loaded the .44, shoved a handful of spare cartridges into a pocket. Then he plunged upward again.

When he reached the tracks, the crackling of the inferno was louder and he could feel its hot breath. Smoke rolled toward him in long, billowing columns. Flames boiled hungrily over a ridge less than half a mile away.

Rudabaugh wedged the revolver down inside his Levi's, held his right arm in tight against his body, and ran past the locomotive and headlong down the center of the tracks.

3

Moving at a slowed trot behind the rest of the pack, Kincaid and seven others carried Honeycutt and Denbow in two-man, five-minute shifts: carry, rest, carry, rest. The men in each team stood shoulder to shoulder, supporting one of the wounded lengthwise across their bodies, the way you'd carry an armload of heavy firewood. Doing it that way allowed them to move straight ahead, conserved some of their flagging strength.

Kincaid had just been relieved again, had come down off the ties to the packed earth of the right-of-way. His arms and legs ached from the strain. Fatigue made him light-headed. They were all near exhaustion. Ahead, people were staggering, swaying drunkenly. Now and then one of them would fall, have to be helped back up. Men supported and half dragged wives and older children carried the younger kids. Silent, all of them—no cries, not even audible whimpers from the youngsters.

How far had they come? Had to be nearly a mile, which meant it was no more than thirty minutes since they'd left the wrecked train. It seemed to Kincaid they had been running for hours; his sense of time was distorted. But the fire hadn't reached the explosives yet—any minute now but not yet—and he judged they were out of immediate danger from the blast. Still, he knew that when the dynamite and black powder did blow, the force of the explosion would hurl burning bits of wood and metal a long way. New blazes would start behind them, on either side. They wouldn't even be near safety until they reached the logging road, and then their survival would depend on where the fire fighters from Springwood and neighboring farms and ranches were situated; on how fast the fire spread after the explosion; on how much strength each of them had left. . . .

Above a series of sawtooth ridges to the east, the sky was stained a deepening ruby color hazed by smoke. The grayness overhead and to the west was tinted with faded blue, but down here the light was uncertain, made murky by tree shadows.

Kincaid dragged an arm across his sweating face, squinted past the ragged line of people. He could make out a downward left-hand turn far ahead; where they were now, the tracks ran in a mostly straight line. He tried to recollect just where the logging road crossed the right-of-way, couldn't seem to visualize it or the terrain near it. No particular landmarks in this area. Just unrelieved wilderness crowding in on both sides.

He gave his attention to Rose. She was still trotting along behind the two men who were carrying Denbow; had been there the whole time, hovering like a wraith. *I've got to stay with him, Matt.* Meaning now, here, until this ordeal was over? Or telling him that she had made her decision, that her husband was the one she'd chosen?

The other carry teams were starting to falter; the five-minute rest period was almost up. Kincaid ran ahead, joined Ashmead this time in carrying the inert body of Sam Honeycutt. The old man's face was gray, waxy; he looked dead. But his chest moved faintly and breath rattled in his throat. The bandaged wound in his shoulder was soaked with fresh blood.

He's not going to make it, Kincaid thought.

Then he thought: Hold on, just hold on! Talking mutely to Honeycutt, and to himself and the others, too.

More long minutes passed. Carry. Rest. Carry. Still no explosion.

Into the downward curves, out of it into another straight, and the same unbroken green and brown stretching out on both sides.

Still no explosion.

The logging road *couldn't* be far ahead now. If they could just get to that road before the fire reached the wrecked train . . .

CHAPTER 17

1

RUDABAUGH ROUNDED ANOTHER TURN IN THE TRACKS, still pounding down the center of the ties. His breath came in ragged gasps. He'd stumbled and fallen a couple of times, lost the Starr .44 once and had to waste seconds retrieving it. But for all of that, he'd managed so far to maintain a steady pace for what must have been almost a mile.

Through a film of sweat he saw that the tracks ahead were still empty. The people from Big Tree must have had a big jump on him; he was moving faster than they'd be able to with the women and kids. He wasn't sure what he'd do if he did catch up to them. Hang back and follow them to the fire lines or into Springwood—and risk being spotted or caught by the fire when the explosives finally blew? Go off into the woods, try to follow along out of sight—and risk getting himself lost?

He just didn't know. He couldn't think straight, with the pain all through him and the blood thudding wildly in his head. A ranch . . . all he had to do was find a ranch . . . there'd be horses, a road, a way out of this trap. . . .

He'd been trapped before, like that time in Emporia, Kansas, when he and the Donegan brothers had gotten themselves boxed into the livery stable after holding up the Cattleman's Bank. Thought he was a goner that day but they'd gotten out of it. Set a fire to get out of that trap, only this time the fire *was* the trap. . . .

He staggered into another curve, halfway out of it. He could feel himself slowing down, starting to wobble; his legs were full of sharp, stinging needles. He had to rest for a few seconds. If he didn't, he knew he would collapse.

Gasping, he pulled up and bent over at the waist and sucked air through his open mouth. After a minute some of the tightness in his chest eased. He forced himself to move again, but he was no longer running—only lurching forward in a loose-gaited trot, like a spavined horse.

Got to be a ranch, got to be a road, got to be a way out—

And the dynamite and black powder blew.

Even though he'd been waiting for it, the sudden booming blast threw him off-stride. The ties under his feet seemed to ripple from the concussion; the shadowy morning turned match-flame bright. There were more explosions, a short chain of them, like mortar shells falling on a target. Rudabaugh regained his balance, lurched around.

The sky behind him was raining fire.

2

Seconds before the explosion, Rose saw the logging road appear ahead of them.

They were just coming through a long bend, and one of the men at the front let out a weak shout. She lifted her head, saw people pointing, heard them calling out, and when she'd run a little farther, there it was, less than a hundred yards away—a rutted brown line that bisected a shallow clearing to the east, climbed across the right-of-way, and vanished into the trees to the west.

The road was empty as far as she could see, but that didn't mean fire fighters weren't somewhere close by. Even if help was a long way off, the road meant safety. She'd been afraid her legs would give out before they reached it, but now, seeing it so close, she knew she had enough strength left to—

The explosion was so sudden and so loud that she threw her hands up to her ears convulsively, to shut out the thunderous noise. All along the tracks people were slowing, turning as she did to look to the north. Black smoke and swirling flame blanketed the sky above the treetops. More smoke and pellets of fire hurtled toward them, out away from them on both sides, as a series of lesser eruptions began.

None of the falling fire reached them, just wispy vanguards of smoke. But burning debris landed on trees no more than a quarter of a mile distant, set them instantly ablaze. Fire raced through the dry top branches, sending up cascades of sparks and cinders. The air turned hot and foul. Rose coughed, then retched.

Someone grabbed her, kept her on her feet. Matt. She sagged against him, let him half carry her onward because her legs simply did not want to work anymore. Her mind was jumbled. She couldn't get enough air into her lungs, could barely see for the sweat streaming into her eyes.

She had a dim awareness of the others running, veering off the right-of-way toward the logging road on the west. The explosions had stopped; she heard only the humming crackle of the fire.

Then they were on the logging road, stumbling down it past a fork, with nothing ahead of them but emptiness. . . .

3

As soon as Rudabaugh saw the firebrands raining down behind him, he forgot all about the pain and broke into a hard run. He ran with his head down and his neck muscles bunched, telling himself the fire wouldn't reach this far, half expecting one of the brands to drop down on him. He could hear the muffled *whoosh* of tree branches igniting. But he didn't look back; he didn't want to know how close the blaze was.

Choking gray-black smoke eddied around him, clogged his nostrils, burned in his throat. He ran blind for more seconds or minutes. Tripped on a warped tie as he came out ahead of the curling tendrils and sprawled out over one of the rails. Hauled himself upright, plunged through another turn and into the next straight stretch.

He didn't see the road until he was within fifty yards of it.

When he did see it, through a blur of sweat, he slowed into a weaving, splayfooted gait. Take the road? But which way? If he took the wrong direction, he might trap himself for fair. *Which way was Springwood?*

He kept on going, trying to make a decision. But his brain wouldn't respond. The roar of the fire, his tortured breathing, his boots thudding against wood and earth, the pound of blood in his ears . . . together they created such a rage of sound that he could no longer think—

There was a man ahead of him.

All at once he was seeing a man run out from the road and up onto the tracks.

He pawed at his eyes, blinking: the man was still there, waving frantically at him, running now in his direction. The hammering in his ears diminished; all his senses came rushing back. He slowed to a walk, then came to a stop. Stood there swaying, sucking air. Inside him was a thin wild laughter.

Not one of the Big Tree people—a fire fighter. And the way out of the trap.

By the time the fire fighter got to him, his mind was working again and he had command of himself. Kid about twenty, with a farmboy look. The kid could tell from the way Rudabaugh was clutching his right arm that he was hurt, so he reached out to take hold of his left arm and steady him. Rudabaugh let the kid do it. He didn't want hands on him, not with the butt of the .44 out where the kid could see it, but he was still too weak to fend him off.

The kid said, "Lordy," in a hushed voice. He was looking at Rudabaugh's face. Then he said, "Take it easy, mister, we'll have you out of here pretty quick."

Rudabaugh cast a look to the north. Smoke curled along the tracks, between the walls of trees. He could see flames leaping skyward above the gray pall, but none of them was an immediate threat.

The kid said, "Anybody else with you?"

The stabbing pain in Rudabaugh's lungs had lessened; his breathing had slowed enough so that he could talk. "No," he managed hoarsely. "Just me."

The kid hurriedly led him down off the right-of-way to the west, onto the logging road. His legs were shaky, full of shooting pains, but he could still walk all right.

"What were those explosions?" the kid asked. "Sounded like a war goin' on."

"Don't know. Listen, where you taking me?"

"Not far. Another road that forks off this one."

"What's there? More fire fighters?"

"Just my pa. We come out to scout the fire, see if we could find out about those explosions. Rest of the men are back a half mile."

"Anybody with your pa?"

"No."

"How'd you come? Horseback?"

"Well, sure not on foot. Pa's holdin' the horses. Don't worry, we'll get you clear."

Rudabaugh wasn't worrying, now that he knew there were horses close by. He said, "How far is Springwood?"

"Couple of miles."

"Along which fork?"

"South one's the fastest way," the kid said. "We got a doc and some volunteer nurses waitin'."

"I don't need a doc."

"You need one, mister."

They were into the woods now. Thin wisps of smoke undulated through the trees around them. More smoke drifted overhead, shutting out part of the morning sky. The thrumming of the blaze seemed farther away now, muffled some by the densely grown timber.

Shortly they reached the fork where a second logging road branched off to the south. An older version of the kid stood off on the south fork, holding a pair of saddle horses—well-trained animals that weren't nearly as skittish as most would have been this near a forest fire.

The older man called something that Rudabaugh didn't listen to. He yanked out of the kid's grasp, stepped back, and dragged the .44 out of his belt with his left hand. The two fire fighters froze in their tracks. Stood staring at him and the revolver, wide-eyed.

"What in hell?" the older one said.

"Don't give me cause, you won't get shot."

"What's the idea throwin' down on us?"

"Shut up. When I come over there, you hand me both reins and then move over next to your son. Don't do anything else or I'll kill you both. Hear?"

The farmer heard and didn't give him any argument. Rudabaugh went over to him and the horses, shifting the .44 to his right hand—he would have had trouble firing it with that hand but they didn't know that—and took hold of both sets of reins with his left. Both animals moved nervously at his unfamiliar nearness, but he knew horses, knew how to handle them. He talked soft to them while the farmer went over to stand beside his son; that kept them from pulling free, bolting.

The leaner, faster-looking, and least skittish of the two was a long-necked claybank. Rudabaugh slid the .44 back inside his Levi's, let go of the other horse's reins, and slapped its rump to send it running away along the west fork. Then he swung himself into the saddle, reined the claybank around to the south.

Neither of the farmers had moved. But the kid shouted, "You got no damn place to go, mister. By Christ, no damn place to go on that horse!"

"Save your breath for running," Rudabaugh said. He sleeved sweat out of his eyes, kicked the claybank into a fast trot down the south fork. When he glanced over his shoulder, he saw the two fire fighters racing after him. But then the horse took him around a bend and he couldn't see them anymore.

At first he had to fight the claybank some to keep it from balking. Soon enough, though, he had it setting a surefooted pace between the ruts. Every jolt of its body sent white-hot pain through his shoulder. He set his teeth, half shut his eyes—enduring it.

Minutes went by, he had no idea how many. Ahead, then, the trees thinned and he could see part of a long, wide meadow where dozens of bare-chested men were working feverishly. Digging firebreaks, he saw as he drew closer.

Fifty or more, giving the meadow the look of a plowed field
with their shovels. The road hooked through the middle of
it, down into a distant valley where buildings squatted in
clusters. Springwood. And beyond Springwood, roads that
would take him out of these mountains and eventually back
to San Francisco.

He fought down the urge to dig his boot heels into the
claybank's flanks, drive the horse at a hard run out of the
woods and across the open meadow. But it would only call
attention to him, invite pursuit. He held the horse down to a
trot as the last of the trees slipped past and they emerged into
pale smoky daylight.

None of the men paid him much mind until he was a third
of the way across the meadow. Then, over on the left, two
of them straightened as he neared. One called suddenly,
"Hey! Hey, you there!"

Rudabaugh kept his eyes front, his left hand holding the
reins in close to the butt of the .44.

The same same voice shouted, "Hey! That's Ed Gorman's
claybank! I'd know that horse anywheres."

"What the hell, mister?" somebody else yelled. "Where's
Ed? What're you doin' with his horse?"

Rigid in the saddle, Rudabaugh realized the mistake he'd
made in his fatigue and urgency—the meaning of the kid's
last words back at the fork: "You got no damn place to go,
mister. By Christ, no damn place to go on that horse." Savagely he drove his heels into the claybank's sides.

But it was already too late.

Three fire fighters surged out onto the road ahead, brandishing shovels. The claybank broke stride, reared sideways.
Rudabaugh fought the reins, tried to bring the animal down
and set him running again. The horse twisted violently
enough to tear the ribbons from Rudabaugh's hand, then
bucked and twisted again. And threw him.

He came down rolling on clumps of turned sod, the
burst of pain in his shoulder making him yell. He fetched
up onto his knees, clawed at his belt. The .44 was gone.
He saw it lying a couple of feet away; lunged for it, caught
it up in his left hand, fired a quick shot—not trying to hit

any of them, just trying to make them scatter so he could run to where several horses were picketed at the far end of the field.

Knowing all the while he'd never make it.

Knowing even before one shovel smashed against his wrist, another against the side of his head, that it was all over now—his luck had finally run out.

4

Kincaid, his arm tight around Rose's shoulders, stumbled along the west fork of the road behind the others. The tops of the trees a few hundred yards back were obscured by great blooms of smoke. Off to the northwest, beyond where the spur tracks ran, colorless flames boiled across the nearest ridge.

Rose was coughing in spasms that shook her body; his own breath wheezed and rattled in his throat. The smoke and the thickness of the woods cast deep hazy shadows over the road. It was like slogging through an evil dream, the kind in which you run and run and never get anywhere.

People ahead were doubled over and weaving erratically; others fell, were helped up. There was panic in all of them again. Now it was driving them onward, but most of them were already at the limits of their endurance.

The road made a sharp hook to the south; the pack leaders disappeared around it. Through burning eyes, Kincaid saw the ones behind the leaders slowing, starting to bunch up across the road. Then some of them turned, gestured with sudden animation at those behind. A weak shout went up.

Kincaid dragged Rose into the turn. And then he, too, could see ahead, far ahead. To where the trees ended. To the open fields stretching away on three sides. To men and animals and wagons, and the buildings of Springwood shimmering to the south like images in a heat mirage.

Rose saw, too. She began to cry without tears.

And Kincaid thought with a sense of wonder: *We made it.*

CHAPTER 18

1

HIS HEAD SWATHED IN BANDAGES, DENBOW LAY ON A COT inside the hospital tent that had been pitched on Springwood's town square. It was night now; he had been awake for about thirty minutes. A lantern burned dimly, so that he could see the half dozen other cots occupied by Big Tree survivors.

One of the volunteer nurses had told him what had happened after the side rod on the Baldwin let go; she'd heard it from some of the others on the train. Miraculously they had all made it to safety, carrying him and Sam Honeycutt for more than a mile, with no fatalities. Even Honeycutt had survived. He was at the local doctor's house, where he could be better cared for, and was given an even chance to live.

The lean stranger had made it here, too. Had been captured by fire fighters when he tried to ride through their lines on a stolen horse, and was now in a cell in the Springwood jail. He hadn't said much, wouldn't even give his name, so nobody knew yet the story behind the boxcars full of weapons and explosives and the blast at the mill.

Firebreaks dug all around Springwood's exposed flanks had kept the blaze from endangering the town. But it was still running wild over east. It would race along for days until it burned itself out, or until the drought broke and rains came. But at least no other community was threatened.

Denbow was thinking about all these things—but mostly

he was thinking about his own actions in the locomotive before the crash. His memory of those hours on the train was vague, dreamlike, as if he had watched it all happen instead of living it. Part of the reason, likely, was the head blow he'd taken, the concussion the nurse had told him he had. But part of it, too, was his mind shying away from what he understood now had been a time of crazy recklessness.

He'd been wrong in nearly everything he had felt and done during that time. Wrong about the Baldwin's capacity to withstand the constant strain of a wide-open throttle. Wrong to have tried once, let alone twice, to disarm the gun-hawk. Wrong about himself. It was funny how you could be so sure of what was right, and then realize later on what a damn fool you'd really been.

What he felt most of all now, lying here, was shame.

It was hot inside the tent, and the flap had been tied back to let in a thin night wind. Through the opening he could see the sky. Clouds, dark and restless, were massing to the west and scudding eastward. Rain clouds—it was going to rain tonight for the first time in over three months.

One day too late, he thought. For him, for everybody from Big Tree—one day too late.

He was still watching the movement of the clouds when a shape appeared in the tent opening, blotting out his view. It was Rose. Dry-mouthed, he watched her enter and glance around, then walk to his cot. She wore a faded calico dress someone must have given her, and her hair was washed clean and brushed and tied back with a blue ribbon. There was a small, grave smile on her mouth as she knelt beside him.

"How do you feel, Will?"

"Poorly. I've a concussion."

"Yes, but it isn't serious. You'll be well again soon."

Denbow cleared his throat. "I know most of what happened, from one of the nurses. We're all lucky to be alive."

"Yes."

"The train wreck was my fault," he said. "Did Kincaid tell you that?"

"No. He didn't say anything about it."

"He was one of those who helped carry me, wasn't he?"

"He was."

Wrong about Kincaid, too.

"It doesn't matter about the wreck," Rose said. "Not now. Everyone is safe—that is what matters."

"I could have killed us all," he said.

"Will . . ."

"I'm not feeling sorry for myself. I'm just stating a fact." He ran his tongue over cracked lips. "I'm not the same man I was, Rose. I reckon none of us are the same. I learned some things last night, but I'm not sure yet what any of them mean."

"Your leg . . . are you still so bitter?"

"Yes," he said, "I'm still bitter. But maybe I can learn to live with it."

"You could still take a job in the Oakland yards. . . ."

"I might. I don't know yet." He looked past her for a time, out again at the scudding black clouds. Then he said, "About us, Rose—we have to talk about us."

"I know. But we don't have to do it now."

"We do," he said. "Right now. It's something we should've done long since. For both our sakes."

2

Kincaid sat alone on the bank of a crooked little stream, listening to the night sounds. Behind him, a few hundred yards away, he could hear voices in the encampment that had been hastily set up for the refugees of Big Tree. Once, a while ago, he had even heard someone laugh again.

But there was no laughter in him. Even though he had slept for ten hours, he was still exhausted; there was still a tautness in him, too. And an emptiness. For he had already reconciled himself to the painful truth that Rose intended to stay with her husband.

Would she be happy with Denbow? Well, she'd been happy with him once—must have been. Denbow was a decent man underneath his bitterness and foolish pride; Kincaid wondered, now, how he could have hated him so much, even for a little while. If Denbow learned to live with his handicap, he'd be a proper husband again. Time was all he needed. Time, and a woman like Rose.

Time would dull his own ache for her, he thought. And when enough of it had passed, he wouldn't even think about her much anymore. Until then he'd find a new place to live and rebuild his life. Start another ranch, maybe, in another small valley. Or, hell, maybe not. Might be best for a man like him just to take a job working for somebody else. If you didn't own much, you couldn't lose much.

The night was sticky-hot; the raw, burned skin under the bandages on his shoulder and chest itched from the sweat. He felt the need of a smoke, but he had no pipe or tobacco. He shifted position on the grassy bank, saw the fireglow staining the whole of the eastern sky a smoky orange, and transferred his gaze to the clouds that had massed to the west.

"Matt?"

He turned so sharply that the bandages pulled and the pain made him wince. She was standing a few feet away. She walked softly; he hadn't even heard her approach.

"What is it, Rose?"

"May I sit down?"

"Might be best if you didn't," he said. "I know why you're here."

"I don't think you do."

"To tell me your decision. But you didn't have to come. I already know what it is."

"I don't think you do," she said again. She came ahead and sat down next to him on the grass. "Will and I have agreed to dissolve our marriage."

He had trouble believing it for a second. He wanted it so much, he was afraid it couldn't be true.

"We had a long talk just now," Rose said. "We decided it was the right thing for both of us. My sister's husband is a lawyer in San Francisco; I'll see him as soon as I can and ask him to begin the proceedings.

"But I thought—" Kincaid broke off, started over. "You went with Will this morning, stayed with him all day—"

"He is still my husband. I *had* to stay with him. And I had to talk to him before I came to you."

"You're sure this is what you want? It won't be easy being a divorced woman. . . ."

"I have no children. Wherever I live until the final decree, no one has to know. Nor afterward, either. Are you trying to discourage me, Matt?"

"No. God, no. It's just that I'm afraid you'll change your mind."

She smiled gently. "I won't change my mind. It has been over between Will and me for a long time. We both knew that and tonight we finally admitted it to each other. He simply doesn't need me anymore."

The ache in Kincaid was different now, warm and sweet. "*I* need you," he said.

A little while later, the breeze from the west sharpened and cooled and brought with it the smell of ozone.

And a little while after that, it began to rain.

About the Author

Bill Pronzini is a well-known critic, novelist, and anthologist. He is the author of QUINCANNON, THE LAST DAYS OF HORSE-SHY HALLORAN, and THE GALLOWS LAND.

Ballantine brings you the best of the West— And the best western authors

---